"I'm not the person you used to know," Nicole said.

Brett jerked his head back, surprised by her candidness.

She pointed at him. "You think I'm responsible for my friend's accident." Her voice had a desperate quality about it. "Or you're wondering if someone had a grudge against me and ran my car off the road, but instead of hurting me, they hurt Missy." Her eyebrow twitched as Nicole seemed to fight back the harsh reality. Missy hadn't simply been hurt.

More than likely, Missy had been killed.

Brett threaded his fingers. "I'm investigating the accident. That's all."

Nicole leaned forward in her chair. "I've changed. Please leave me alone." She started to get up. Brett's hand on hers stopped her. Their gazes met and lingered.

"Someone wanted your car to go into the lake." He leaned in closer. *"Your car."*

Nicole clutched her mittens in her hand. "You really think someone wanted to hurt me?" She let out a mirthless laugh. "I lead a pretty quiet life."

"You didn't always lead a quiet life."

Books by Alison Stone

Love Inspired Suspense

Plain Pursuit
Critical Diagnosis
Silver Lake Secrets

ALISON STONE

left snowy Buffalo, New York, and headed a thousand miles south to earn an industrial engineering degree at Georgia Tech in Hotlanta. Go Yellow Jackets! She loved the South, but true love brought her back north.

After the birth of her second child, Alison left corporate America for full-time motherhood. She credits an advertisement to write children's books for sparking her interest in writing. She never did complete a children's book, but she did have success writing articles for local publications before finding her true calling, writing romantic suspense.

Alison lives with her husband of more than twenty years and their four children in western New York, where the summers are absolutely gorgeous and the winters are perfect for curling up with a good book—or writing one.

Besides writing, Alison keeps busy volunteering at her children's schools, driving her girls to dance and watching her boys race motocross.

Alison loves to hear from her readers at Alison@AlisonStone.com. For more information please visit her website, www.alisonstone.com. She's also chatty on Twitter, @Alison_Stone. If you're on Facebook, find her at
www.facebook.com/AlisonStoneAuthor.

Read 12-16-2017 _SJS_

SILVER LAKE
SECRETS

ALISON STONE

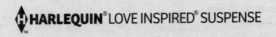
HARLEQUIN® LOVE INSPIRED® SUSPENSE

™ LOVE INSPIRED BOOKS

ISBN-13: 978-0-373-44640-7

Silver Lake Secrets

www.Harlequin.com

Printed in U.S.A.

Redemption does not come so easily,
for no one can ever pay enough to live forever
and never see the grave.
—*Psalms* 49:8–9

To my big sister, Annie St. George.
(You will always be Ann Marie to me.)
Thanks for the insight into the glamorous world
of funeral homes. I figure your numerous career
choices over the years are good for
at least a few more books. Love you.

To my husband, Scott,
and my children, Scotty, Alex, Kelsey and Leah.
Love you always and forever.

ONE

The whirring of the tow truck's motor sliced through the cold, eerie silence. A thin layer of ice coated the freshly fallen snow. Chief Brett Eggert chose his steps carefully as he walked along the curved country road. Head bent against the blinding snowstorm, he examined the quickly disappearing tire tracks that left the road at the curve and vanished into the black, murky water through an ominous opening in an otherwise frozen lake.

Not a good sign.

The red and white flashing lights of Silver Lake's rescue vehicles—all three of them—swept across the dark form of the lone diver waist-deep in the frigid water. If the diver drifted away from the ring of artificial light, the black night would swallow him. A chill skittered down Brett's spine. He stuffed his hands into the pockets of his lined jacket, relieved and guilt-ridden that it wasn't him outfitted in a wet suit performing the search and rescue.

"Please let it be a rescue," he muttered to himself.

The rugged soles of Brett's boots fought for purchase on the icy incline as he navigated his way to the edge of the lake. There, Officer Ed Hanson, forehead wrinkled in concentration, took copious notes on a thick stack of papers on a police-issue clipboard. Brett suspected the young officer had missed his calling as a novelist.

"Chief." Ed's eyebrows shot up and the lines eased from his face. He pointed his pen toward the road. "Tracks indicate car missed the curve. Tough to tell more than that.

This beast of a snowstorm is messing with my accident scene."

"Any victims?"

"Car was empty." Ed brushed the snow from his paperwork and made another note.

Those three simple words pinged in Brett's brain. "What happened to the driver?"

"The dive team's still searching." Ed scrubbed his leather glove across his face, his nose red from the punishing lake winds. "The water's moving quickly. Afraid the driver might have exited the vehicle and been swept away." Ed's confident tone slipped on the last word. Perhaps because he didn't want to believe the driver had perished in the accident.

The tow truck's motor whined at a higher pitch. The bumper of a Nissan Cube broke through the surface. Sludgy brownish-green water sluiced down its sides and apprehension pricked the back of Brett's neck.

He knew that car. His stomach pitched as he ran his cold fingers over his lips.

The driver was missing.

Ed jabbed his pen in the direction of the vehicle. "Isn't that…? I've seen that car around town." He turned to face Brett. "You know who I'm talking about, right?"

Fear burned Brett's gut like a bowl of diner chili on a midshift break. "Yeah. I know that car." He cleared his throat, hoping he could keep his voice steady. "I believe Nicole Braun drives a lime-green Nissan Cube."

Ed pushed his hat up on his forehead. "I've seen her around town a few times. She had a kid with her. Oh, man…" he added, as if he had just realized the missing driver was a mom who might have had a young passenger.

"Any sign of a child on the scene?"

"No, sir."

Brett had never heard about a child. Maybe Ed was mistaken. And if Brett hadn't seen Nicole around town himself a few times over the past few months, he might have assumed Ed was mistaken that this was Nicole's car, too. When Nicole had left town years ago as a teenager, Brett figured she'd never return to Silver Lake.

Considering this tragic twist, Brett wished she had never returned.

Ed angled his body away from Brett and the punishing winds to call in the license plate. Brett stared at the vehicle, wondering what Nicole had been up to since she left Silver Lake. Unexplainable regret wormed its way into his gut now that he'd probably never find out.

Ed pulled the phone away from his ear. "The plates are registered to Nicole A. Braun."

Brett shook his head and the pain in his gut showed no sign of letting up. Sometimes he hated his job.

Really hated his job.

Brett scanned the snow for footprints, but realized he'd never be able to discern Nicole's prints from those of the rescue personnel.

If she had gotten out.

"Any chance the driver made it to safety?" A sliver of hope splintered the shell around his heart. The shell that protected him from the darkness threatening to crowd in on him. A person couldn't do this job without coping mechanisms.

Part of him wondered why he cared. Nicole had been nothing but a source of misery to his family. Yet he took strange solace in knowing he hadn't lost all compassion in the course of doing a tough job.

Brett was empathetic, or so he tried to convince himself, but familiar anger and emptiness swirled inside him at the thought of Nicole. He scanned the murky water and the fine hairs at the back of his neck prickled to life.

He'd never wished her dead.

"She'd be soaking wet if she made it to shore. She couldn't go far." Ed squinted against the snowflakes.

"*She* has a name. Nicole Braun."

The officer gave him a subtle nod. "If Miss Braun had made it to safety, she would have gone to the closest house." Ed jerked his chin toward a well-maintained home overlooking the lake. "Mr. Hendricks, the neighbor who called us, is home. He would have been there to answer the door.

"Mr. Hendricks was a little uncertain about what happened. He thought he saw two sets of headlights coming around the curve with one vehicle missing the curve." Ed gestured with his thumb toward the water. "It ended up here. It's been snowing pretty hard. The more I talked to the witness, the more he started to wonder if he had seen only one car. The headlights bounce off the falling snow. Either way, good thing he witnessed the accident. Miss Braun's car could have gone unreported for...I don't know how long."

"No one else reported an accident?" Not one car had passed since Brett had arrived.

"No. Afraid not."

Brett nodded, staring at the mud-caked wheel wells of the Cube. The tow truck's spotlight lit on a fish magnet on the back of the car. Nicole didn't seem the type. Had she truly changed that much since her wild teenage years?

He scratched his head. What did it matter now?

If he believed in God and heaven and all that stuff—stuff his parents had shoved down his throat to the point he wanted to puke—it might have been a source of comfort. A sign she believed.

Now, it only made him doubt everything he had thought he knew about his deceased brother's girlfriend.

Brett ran a hand along his jaw. He stared at the vehicle

as the tow truck driver secured it to the back of the truck. "I'll contact the family."

Ed cut him a sideways glance. "You sure you're up for that? I understand—"

Brett held up his hand. There were many benefits of living in a small town, but everyone knowing when a guy blew his nose wasn't one of them. "I got it."

Ed met his gaze, then nodded like the good subordinate he was.

Brett turned on his heel and hiked up the incline. The icy snow crunched under his boots. He lost his footing once and had to put his hand down to catch himself. At times like these, he wondered why he hadn't moved south, away from the harsh winters of Western New York.

He climbed behind the wheel of his cruiser, cranked up the heat and squeezed the cool leather of the steering wheel. He stared straight ahead at the swirling snowstorm.

This couldn't be happening.

Hard to imagine that now, eight years later, Nicole had met the same fate as his brother—both their lives snuffed out in horrific car accidents.

Brett plodded through the six inches of fresh snow covering the front walk leading to Miss Mary's small ranch. He wrapped his gloved hand around the black metal railing, steeling himself against the onslaught of emotion clogging his throat. Notifying families of accidents—possibly fatal—was never easy.

Brett took off his hat and tucked it under his arm. He pressed the cracked doorbell and waited. And listened. He drew in a deep breath and let it out, trying to even his emotions.

Nicole's grandmother had been confined to a wheel-chair recently, the reason, as he understood, Nicole had returned to Silver Lake. A sense of anticipation flooded his gut and made him antsy.

Patience.

Navigating a wheelchair through the small house would take a little extra time. He blew out a few short breaths. The moment Miss Mary opened the door, her life would be changed. Forever. No going back. He ran a hand across his short-cropped hair and mentally rehearsed the few feeble words of comfort he planned to offer.

The door creaked open. Brett glanced down, anticipating Miss Mary's sweet face looking up at him from a wheelchair. The same sweet face that, a lifetime ago, made Sunday-school lessons fun. To his surprise, a little boy with hazel eyes, a splash of freckles across his nose and a quizzical expression on his face appeared in the doorway. Something distant, like a forgotten memory, whispered across his brain.

"Hi, mister." The little boy's voice snapped Brett back to the moment.

Brett crouched to the level of the boy. "Is your grandma home?" The word *grandma* came out as a question.

The boy glanced over his shoulder but didn't open the door more than a foot. He was probably cold in his super-hero pj's and bare feet. "My Gigi's home."

"Your great grandmother?"

The little boy nodded slowly.

Of course.

"Can you get her?" Brett forced a smile, his lips and cheeks frozen from the elements.

Footsteps sounded down the hall and Brett narrowed his gaze.

The door flew open. A wash of confusion mixed with relief swept over him. Dressed in gray sweats, with her long, wavy brown hair flowing over her shoulders, Nicole

Braun glared at him, the annoyance in her gaze matching her tone. "Can I help you?"

Max's brother stood at her door.

Nicole braced her hand against the door frame, pinpricks of anxiety sweeping up her arms. An officer at the door with his hat tucked under his arm was not a positive development, especially when the officer happened to be the older brother of her deceased boyfriend. She swallowed hard and her eyes drifted down to her son.

She nudged Ethan's arm. "Run and tell Gigi I'll be back in a few minutes with her tea."

Ethan glanced at the officer with wide eyes. Her little man was at the age when a man in uniform was automatically a hero. "Aw, Mom," he groaned. "Can't I stay?"

Nicole's gaze landed on the man standing on her porch. Flecks of gold touched his brown eyes, just as they did in her son's.

Just like Max's eyes.

She tucked a strand of hair behind her ear then crossed her arms in front of her and stifled a shudder, thankful she could blame it on the arctic wind whipping in through the open door.

The officer's unreadable expression did nothing to quell her rioting emotions. Had he uncovered her secret? Nicole placed a possessive hand on Ethan's shoulder. "Go." Impatience and dread weighed heavily on her chest.

Once her son was out of earshot, she leaned her hip against the door frame and forced a curt tone. "Can I help you?" She made a big show of letting her gaze drop to his name tag. "Chief Brett Eggert." But she knew exactly who he was.

Who his family was.

Who his brother was.

Or had been.

Nicole glanced over her shoulder to make doubly sure Ethan had followed her instructions. She didn't want him to overhear their conversation.

"Nicole." He tipped his head in greeting. "It's me, Brett. Max's brother."

"I know who you are, Chief Eggert." She made sure her voice oozed with indifference.

A hint of confusion creased the corners of his eyes. "You can call me Brett."

She crossed her arms and sighed. "Okay, what do you want, *Brett*?" Despite her snarky attitude, her nerves hummed with apprehension. She had no idea why he was here—but she wasn't about to show any weakness in front of an Eggert, a member of the family that had run her out of town eight years ago.

Brett seemed to do a mental shake and something flittered across his eyes. "Were you in an accident this evening?"

She slowly shook her head. "I don't even have my..." She was about to say the word *car*, when it hit her. Cold icy fear pumped through her veins, matching the chill on her flesh. "My friend Missy Flowers borrowed my car." Her eyes widened. "Has there been an accident? Is she okay?" Instinctively she sent up a quick prayer for her friend.

But why was he asking her if she had been in an accident? If Missy was okay, he would have known Nicole wasn't driving her own car. Her stomach pitched and her mind scrambled with the possibilities. Nothing made sense.

Nicole stepped back and held out her arm, suddenly forgetting all the reasons she shouldn't invite this man into her home. "Come in." The words rasped in her dry throat.

"Is Missy okay?" she asked again, her impatience growing each time he didn't answer her question.

Brett stepped into the foyer, his broad shoulders filling the narrow space. His silence ramped up her panic.

Dear Lord, let Missy be okay, she repeated in her head. *Please, please, please.*

"We pulled your vehicle out of the lake this evening."

"And Missy...?" Blackness darkened the periphery of her vision. She flattened her palm against the flowered wallpaper. "Is Missy okay? I let her borrow my car." A shrill tone laced the edges of her words. She fisted her hands at her side, resisting the urge to reach out and throttle him. Demand some reassurance.

His somber expression gave none.

"I'm sorry," he finally said, his voice gruff. "No one was in the car."

Nicole's brow furrowed. "No one? How can that be? Where's Missy?" The busy wallpaper swirled and the ground heaved underneath her.

This wasn't the first time an officer had notified her of a traffic accident. The night the police officer came to her door to tell her Max had been killed in a wreck was imprinted on her brain. She'd never forget that night and the subsequent tailspin it had sent the rest of her life into.

Dragging her hand along the wall, she tottered to the kitchen. She found her purse hanging on the back of a chair. Her pulse roared through her ears competing with the *Jeopardy!* theme music in the next room. She clawed through her purse until she found her cell phone.

Brett was saying something—headlights, accident, gone—but his words sounded like they were being forced through a long tunnel like thick goop. The orange and brown hues of her grandmother's dated kitchen sharpened into focus.

"I'll call Missy. Maybe...somehow..." She swiped a finger across the smudged screen of her smartphone. Nicole frantically entered her passcode. She tried three times before she got it right. She dialed her friend's number and lifted her eyes to meet Brett's while the phone rang. *Once...twice...* His sympathetic expression made it difficult for her to breathe.

Nicole studied the floor and focused all her energy on the ringing phone.

Three...four...five...

She imagined Missy clawing through her oversize bag, muttering to herself, fumbling for her cell phone. In one second Missy would answer and someday they'd laugh and laugh about the time she borrowed Nicole's car and drove it into the lake during a snowstorm. Yeah. Ha-ha.

Missy's cheerful voice sounded on the line. "It's me. You know what to do." Voice mail.

The last shred of hope drained from Nicole's numb limbs. "Missy, call me as soon as you get this. I'm worried about you. Really worried..." Her last word crumbled on a sob. She tossed the phone down on the table and dropped into a chair, its legs skidding on the worn linoleum floor. "She's not going to call me, is she?"

"The circumstances seem dire." Brett stood in the middle of her kitchen, as if frozen, unwilling to commit to an answer. He cleared his throat. "How do you know Missy?"

"We both work at the funeral home." Nicole pressed her palms together and touched the tip of her nose with her fingers. "I told her not to go to Buffalo. That the weather was bad." She bit her lower lip, fearing she'd lose it if she let herself cry. "I canceled an appointment I had in Buffalo tonight. We were supposed to go into Buffalo together. Me for my meeting. Missy to visit a boyfriend. But my grandmother wasn't feeling well. I didn't want to leave her alone with my son." She winced, wondering if she had made a mistake by mentioning her son, but hiding Ethan's paternity when her friend was missing didn't exactly seem to be a top priority.

Nicole continued, "Missy was determined to see her boyfriend and she doesn't have a car." Her friend had an infectious smile and could talk anyone into anything, including talking Nicole into lending out her car on a snowy night, against her better judgment.

"Where was Missy headed?" Brett sat across from Nicole.

"Her boyfriend lives outside of Buffalo." Nicole rested her elbows on the table and stared out the window, willing her car to appear in its usual spot in the driveway. "How could this be happening?"

"The lake is mostly frozen, but there are strong undercurrents. The dive team is still searching...I'm sorry." Brett paused, the compassion in his voice both comforting and unnerving. She wanted someone to reassure her that Missy was fine, not apologize for the reasons she wasn't. "What time did Missy leave Silver Lake?"

She glanced at the bird clock on the wall and saw it was about to chirp the eight o'clock hour. She sighed. "About two hours ago. I know because I was supposed to meet..." She hesitated, uncertain how much she wanted to say "...I had planned to meet with a client of the funeral home to straighten out some paperwork."

She traced a scar on her grandmother's oak kitchen table. "I had to cancel my plans because my grandmother wasn't feeling well. The meeting could wait." She hoped. A funeral home client had complained he hadn't received the services his father had paid for prior to his burial. Isaac King had threatened to file a complaint with the Better Business Bureau, his lawyer and anyone who would listen if his complaint wasn't resolved in a timely manner.

Nicole did some office work and cosmetology at the funeral home. When she answered Mr. King's angry call, she promised to meet with him. Hopefully to clear things up. She didn't want to bother Mr. Peters with this. He had enough on his plate caring for his ailing wife. Ultimately, it came down to two things: Peters Funeral Home couldn't afford the bad publicity and Nicole couldn't afford to lose her job.

"A storm was blowing in. Wasn't Missy worried about driving in the snow?" Brett's question snapped her back to the moment.

Nicole traced the scar on the table's surface in the reverse direction. "Missy grew up in Buffalo. She was used to driving in the snow." Nicole shrugged. "Maybe she was a little too confident."

Nicole rested her chin on the palm of her hand. "The weather forecasters around here are always calling for a snow Armageddon. It never materializes. The weather probably caught her off guard." A small part of her was cognizant of the ridiculousness of talking about the weather, but she couldn't think straight. "Did you search the area around the lake? Maybe she's confused, wandering around in a state of shock." An ember of hope sparked in her heart. "I'll help. I'll grab my coat."

Brett touched her arm, forcing her to sit back down. "The officers are searching the area, but it's more likely she…" He seemed to be searching for the right words. "Nicole, you need to brace for the worst."

Nicole felt her lower lip begin to quiver. She didn't *want* to brace for the worst. She wanted to have hope. Hope that God had protected Missy.

"Was Missy under the influence of anything when she left?"

Anger, hot and unexpected, swept up her neck and cheeks. "Oh, sure, I'm going to hand over the keys to my car to someone who had been drinking." She leaned in close and whispered, "Don't judge me or my friends by who you think I am. I'm not the same person who left Silver Lake."

Nicole couldn't be sure, but she thought she detected a hint of contrition in his eyes. "I had to ask."

Nicole scratched her head. The anger drifted away, forced out by her growing fear.

"Can I call someone for you?"

"No." Other than her grandmother, her son and her work, she lived in a pretty small bubble. And she liked it that way.

"We'll send an officer to Missy's family. It's just her mother, right? Do you have her information?

"Her mother's name is Gloria. She'd call her by her first name. You know, the way people sometimes do when they're being overly dramatic. She lives in Buffalo. Near the university."

"Okay." Brett patted her hand. "We can track her down. Do you know the contact information for Missy's boyfriend?"

Nicole shook her head. "If I had her cell phone…" The cell phone that was probably at the bottom of the lake. She met Brett's gaze and wrapped her hands tightly around the edge of her seat. None of this seemed real. "Is there something you're not telling me?"

A creak drew her attention toward the TV room. A frail-looking Gigi stopped in the archway, her hand on the wheel of her wheelchair. Her grandmother gave Brett a pointed glare that accentuated the lines around her mouth. "I hope you're not here bothering my granddaughter. She's done nothing wrong. She's here helping me until I can get around on my own again."

A flicker akin to shame flashed across Brett's warm eyes. "No, Miss Mary—"

"Everyone calls me Gigi now."

"Well, I'm afraid I have bad news."

Gigi cocked her head, anticipation on her face.

"Nicole's car was found submerged in the lake."

Her grandmother squared her shoulders and pressed the button on the arm of her wheelchair to set it in motion. When she reached the kitchen table, she put her hand on Nicole's. "Oh, dear. Is Missy okay?"

"Chief Eggert thinks Missy may have skidded off the road in the snow." An ache grew more powerful in the back of Nicole's throat.

"There's something else," Brett said.

Nicole's heart pounded in her ears. She swallowed around a knot in her throat.

"A witness thought he saw two cars coming around the curve. It was snowing heavily at the time, but if there were two cars, one may have pushed your car off the road."

Her grandmother gasped and all the color drained from her face.

Panic crushed Nicole's chest and she struggled to draw breath. "Why would someone do that?"

"That's what we're trying to figure out. Do you have any enemies, Nicole?"

She met his gaze and didn't know what to feel. Brett knew as well as she that the Eggert family hated her. Something unspoken hung in the air.

Nicole ran a hand through her hair. "I've kept to myself since returning to Silver Lake. I've put my past behind me. I haven't kept in touch with anyone from that time in my life. Now, I work and I spend time with my family. That's it."

A thought bothered Nicole. She had planned to meet with Mr. King, the disgruntled funeral home client, in person and compare his contract with the one she'd pulled from the files. What if someone didn't want her to go to that meeting? She shook away the thought. *Ridiculous.*

No, she didn't have any new enemies.

Just the Eggert family, who blamed her for Max's death.

And the drug dealer she had testified against. But he was in prison.

"Do you know if Missy was an aggressive driver? Perhaps the accident was the result of road rage. Or not taking care on snow-covered roads."

Nicole shook her head adamantly. "Never. She'd pick up Ethan from school for me sometimes. I'd never let my son ride in a car if I suspected he wasn't safe."

Brett tapped his hand on the table and stood. "I'm very sorry about your friend."

"Thank you."

"I'll be in touch about your vehicle." He placed his business card on the table.

"I'm not worried about my car. Please call me when you find Missy." She tore off a corner of an envelope and scratched down her number. On the way to the front door she handed the paper to him. "Call me the second you find Missy."

Nicole closed the door tightly behind Brett and leaned her forehead against the cool wood.

Ethan ran down the hall and wrapped his arms around her legs. "I want to be a policeman."

Nicole smiled, a strained gesture. Her heart ached. "Chief Eggert is the chief of police. He stopped by, but everything is okay." She tousled his hair. *Everything is going to be okay. Please, Lord, let everything be okay.*

Ethan shrugged, the way kids do. He grabbed his skateboard which had been propped up against the wall. He sat down on it and rolled across the hardwood floor, already marred from fifty years of living. She opened her mouth to yell at him, but stopped. No, today was a day to be thankful. She had another day to spend with Ethan.

Guilt gave a hard edge to her sweet relief.

What if Nicole had been with Missy?

Submerged in the murky depths of Silver Lake.

TWO

Nicole slipped off her long winter coat and hung it on the closet rod inside the funeral home foyer. Missy's fuzzy pink jacket hung in the far corner. A sudden bubble of hope bloomed inside Nicole and then popped.

No, her friend wasn't running the vacuum or dusting some dark corner of the funeral home before she headed to her other cleaning jobs for those wealthy enough to pay for it. No, her friend had forgotten her jacket here yesterday and had asked to borrow Nicole's along with her car last night.

How Missy had left her winter jacket at work on a freezing afternoon was beyond Nicole. Missy often claimed she'd get hot and sweaty doing her job and walk out without it. Happy, carefree and a tad forgetful. That was Missy.

Nicole drew in a deep breath trying to settle her prickly nerves. The walk here had done nothing to expend her nervous energy. The sweet smell of flowers and a faint whiff of lemon dusting spray always struck her when she entered through the front door. But the funky smell was a small price to pay for working primarily in solitude. She thrived on peace and quiet.

Except today. Today Nicole wished Missy would appear with her headphones and vacuum, cracking her pink bubblegum. Her friend was an otherwise bright spot in a gloomy business.

Nicole shoved her pink mittens deep into her coat pockets. She'd be heartbroken if she lost the only material thing connecting her to her mother. Not quite ready to face the day, she slowly walked toward Missy's jacket and tenderly ran her fingers down its fuzzy sleeves, releasing the scent of laundry detergent. Nicole closed her eyes and drew in a deep breath. Today was going to be so much harder than she ever imagined.

Mr. Peters called to her from his office, snapping her out of her maudlin thoughts. She pushed back her shoulders and strode to the doorway so he wouldn't have to get up. He seemed to be moving a lot slower these days. He smiled at her when she entered his office, but his normally bright blue eyes seemed dull. Mr. Peters had been drained from caring for his ailing wife. Today, he appeared even more exhausted, probably after learning about Missy's accident from Brett. Nicole let out a long sigh. She was grateful to Brett for making that difficult call.

Across her boss's messy desk, he handed her a manila file folder. "Here's Mrs. Fenster's folder." The newly deceased. "She needs to be ready for a four o'clock wake."

"Okay." Nicole took the folder and hugged it to her chest. "You okay, Mr. Peters? You look tired."

He lifted a bushy eyebrow. "My wife had a rough night last night. The nurse only comes during the day. I'll have to hire a night nurse, too." A deep line marred his forehead. "If I plan to sleep, that is." He scrubbed a hand over his eyes. "And then I get a call this morning that Missy has gone missing." He shook his head. "I can't imagine what her family is going through right now."

Nicole bit her lower lip. She didn't want to imagine Mrs. Flowers's grief.

Mr. Peters lifted his gaze and studied Nicole. "You and Missy were close, weren't you?"

Something about the way he said *were* made her bristle. "Yes, we are. We became fast friends these past few months. I pray she'll be found safe."

Mr. Peters folded his hands in a solemn gesture. "Yes, it's best to pray at times like these."

Nicole traced the edge of the manila folder with her index finger. "Guess I better tend to—" she read the name on the folder's tab written in Mr. Peters's neat penmanship "—Mrs. Fenster."

"Thank you." Mr. Peters let out a heavy sigh and settled back into his leather chair. A faraway look glossed his eyes. "I hope they find Missy."

"Me, too," Nicole muttered on her way out of the office. She figured the sooner she got lost in her work, the sooner she could have some peace of mind. At least temporarily.

The fax machine in the small office near the top of the basement stairs hummed to life. Curious, Nicole ducked into the room where she normally did some light paperwork. Standing over the machine, she read the paper inching out of the machine. Her throat grew dry. The document was from Isaac King, the son of Abe King. Nicole held her breath while the document finished printing. She folded it and stuffed it into her purse, eager to compare Isaac's copy of the contract with the one she had pulled from the files yesterday afternoon. She hoped she could straighten out this misunderstanding without bothering the already stressed Mr. Peters. In the meantime, she couldn't help but wonder what Mr. Peters would do if he found both the documents wadded up in her designer knock-off purse.

She hustled down a flight of stairs leading to the basement and paused at the landing. Someone had propped open the side door, probably while carrying in a floral arrangement. Rubbing one arm briskly, she groaned and pulled the door closed. The basement was cold enough without letting in an arctic blast.

Nicole descended the rest of the stairs and pushed open the solid basement door, letting the cool air swirl around her ankles. The door slammed behind her. She shuddered.

She loved helping the deceased look their best, but she never quite got used to working in the basement.

Heart pounding in her ears, she hurried to the empty steel table in the corner, spread the fax out and compared it to the original document. According to the undated document from Isaac King, his father had made prearrangements and paid for a top-of-the-line casket. The contract from the file specified a less expensive casket. Less expensive by several thousand dollars.

Her stomach sank.

Both documents had Derreck Denner's flashy signature. Derreck was Mr. Peters's nephew and had come on board about a year ago. Did Derreck change the document of his own accord or had Mr. King made the changes and forgotten to give the new contract to his family before he passed away? She lifted the original document to her face and studied Derreck's signature. She was no expert, but both signatures seemed the same. She held the paper to the light. It was thin. Thin enough for someone to trace a signature.

Nicole tucked a strand of hair behind her ear and racked her brain. Did she think she was a detective now? She shook her head. Maybe it was just a matter of showing Mr. King the document on file, the document that listed a less expensive casket. She threaded her fingers through her hair. Which document was more current? She pounded down the corner of the crumpled documents.

"I should have told Mr. Peters the minute the phone call came in," she muttered to herself.

You were trying to save him the hassle.

Now she had one royal mess on her hands. How could she bring this up to Mr. Peters without seeming as though she was interfering?

Nicole bit her bottom lip. She closed her eyes and rolled her shoulders. It's Derreck's signature on both contracts.

She couldn't exactly accuse Derreck of mishandling a client's money. She had no proof. Her stomach flip-flopped. But why did she have this uneasy feeling? Was it because she had overheard Derreck trying to smooth things over with another disgruntled client a few weeks ago? Or because she had totally bungled her dealings with the King family?

Either way, she'd have to tell Mr. Peters…once she got up the nerve. Then she'd explain how she was trying to help and how she'd never overreach her job description again. *There*. She had a plan. She folded up the two documents and stuffed them into her purse.

Nicole pulled up a stool to her workstation and opened the deceased's file. "Okay, Mrs. Fenster," she spoke aloud to the empty room, a habit she had gotten into when she first started this job six months ago. "You're going to look beautiful, just like you did in—" she picked up the photo of the woman from the file in front of her and studied the black-and-white photo of a woman in a bouffant hairstyle and pillbox hat "—1962."

It amazed Nicole how many family members provided dated photos of the deceased, no doubt at the request of their dearly departed. She supposed everyone wanted to be remembered as they'd appeared in their prime.

Nicole decided that when she died she wouldn't care how she looked.

A muted shuffling made her scalp prickle. She enjoyed the solitude of working alone, she just wished it wasn't in the basement of a funeral home. Her mind tended to play tricks on her. Her gaze drifted to her purse on the steel counter.

Focus on work.

Nicole grabbed her metal makeup box from the cabinet over the sink and set about getting Mrs. Fenster ready for the four o'clock viewing. She sat on the stool and lined up the makeup on a tray.

Another sound, more distinct this time, made her pause and turn toward the basement door. A thin line of light shone around the heavy basement door before it clicked solidly closed. A blanket of goose bumps covered her skin. She set a makeup brush on the tray and squinted into the shadows.

"Who's there?"

The shadows moved and Gene Gentry stepped into the soft light surrounding her workstation. He held a white garbage bag and wore his perpetual apologetic look. Gene was thin with a stooped posture curving his six-foot-six frame. If someone was searching under funeral home embalmer from central casting, they would have found a photo of Gene. His awkward demeanor was perfect for working with the dead, not so much for those they left behind.

"Sorry, Miss Nicole, just emptying the garbage can."

She forced a laugh that echoed in the cavernous space. "It's okay, Gene. Sometimes I let my imagination get the best of me when I'm down here."

Gene fingered the white plastic of the garbage bag. "After a while, you get used to creepy." He snapped the bag to open it and lined the garbage can. He looked up. Nicole thought she detected a hopeful expression. "Do you think you'll stick around?"

"I plan to." Nicole dug through her makeup kit, searching for the blue eye shadow.

"Not exactly where you expected to be working when you graduated high school, huh?" He dragged his fingers over a thinning comb-over that made him appear older than he was. She vaguely remembered him graduating a year ahead of her, or maybe behind. She didn't exactly reminisce about her high school days. And Gene wasn't exactly the kind of person she would have hung around with.

"I'm happy to have the job." She smiled at him, secretly ashamed she hadn't been a model Christian as a teen. But that was a long time ago. She had long since made peace with her past and did her best moving forward. She plucked the blue eye shadow from the bottom of her makeup kit and held it up. "I better get back to work."

"Me, too." Gene lowered his eyes and took a step toward the door, then turned back around. "I'm real sorry about Missy." He cleared his throat. "I sure hope they find her."

Nicole smiled tightly at Gene, trying to hold her emotions at bay. "Pray they find her." Her dark thoughts threatened to smother her. *Keep praying.*

"One time on TV, I saw a tool you should have in your car to break the window if your car goes into the water. Did you have that tool in your car?"

Nicole shook her head. "No, I didn't. But we can't give up hope." Her pulse throbbed in her ears. Hot tears burned the backs of her eyes and blurred the eye shadow palette in front of her. "Well, I really have to get Mrs. Fenster's hair and makeup done."

Gene's eyebrows disappeared under his bangs. "Okay, I'll get going then."

"Have a good day." She watched him slip out of the room, his posture reminiscent of a boy who had been scolded.

Nicole slipped Mrs. Fenster's paperwork into the folder and placed it on the steel table next to her purse. It had taken her a little longer than she had anticipated to get the woman's hair just right.

She snapped her makeup case closed and returned it to the cabinet over the sink. While at cosmetology school,

Nicole had envisioned herself working in a swanky salon in the city where she'd make big tips. When she had returned to Silver Lake to help out her grandmother, visions of a job in a salon vanished. She refused to work where she'd be the subject of gossip.

Now her clients didn't talk or give tips, unless they were of the life-lesson variety, such as "don't eat too much fried food" and "don't cross against the light."

Nicole washed her hands and dried them on a piece of paper towel. She tossed the crumpled-up towel into the wastebasket and wondered if she should do the same with the conflicting documents in her purse.

Mr. King wouldn't forget as easily.

Nicole hiked her purse straps over her shoulder. She'd grab some lunch in the break room and then do some bookkeeping. Maybe if Derreck still wasn't around, she'd finally talk to Mr. Peters so she could put this mess behind her.

Nicole emerged from the basement and slowed at the top of the stairs at the sound of Brett's voice. Panic swept over her, heating every inch of her skin. Had Brett come to report news of Missy? Nicole peeked around the corner and saw Brett standing in Derreck's office doorway. *So much for talking to Mr. Peters in private.* She flattened against the wall so she could listen without detection.

"Do you know much about Melissa Flowers?" Brett asked.

"Sure, Missy's been here a long time. My uncle hired her right out of high school. She always did a good job. Maybe a little too chatty when she should have been doing her job."

Nicole envisioned Derreck, elbows propped on his desk, tapping the pads of his fingers together in an oh-so-thoughtful gesture. "But she got the cleaning done. Missy was a good employee."

Derreck's choice of words pinged around her brain. *Missy was...*

Missy *is, is, is,* she wanted to scream.

"We're terribly worried about her. We're like family at Peters Funeral Home." Derreck's tone oozed just the right amount of concern. The same tone he used on the deceased's relatives, a mix of sympathy and smooth sales-manship. He seemed to be able to turn it on and off at will. "Still no sign of our Missy?"

"I'm afraid not." Brett's voice grew louder, as if he had turned to check the hallway. "Did Missy have any prob-lems? Perhaps here at work?"

Nicole's heartbeat drummed loudly in her ears. She took another step back and bumped into the hall table. The antique vase wobbled. She grabbed the vase to steady it.

Pushing her shoulders back, she strode down the hall, acting as if she hadn't been eavesdropping. She smiled tightly at Brett and nodded toward Derreck, seated be-hind his large mahogany desk, fingers steepled, match-ing her mental image.

"Missy seemed happy. No problems," Derreck said. "Wouldn't you agree, Nicole?"

Nicole slowed her pace and turned toward the office, hoping her cheeks weren't as red as they felt. No one knew about the incriminating papers she had stashed in her purse, so she didn't need to act guilty.

"Yes." She cleared her throat and crossed her arms, un-crossed them and crossed them again. She adjusted her stance. "Missy is a happy person. She never complains about work. She's happy to be employed. Not only does she clean for the funeral home, but several residents in Silver Lake, including your aunt and uncle. It's tough in this economy."

Derreck laughed, an awkward sound considering the circumstances. "How true. Small towns were especially hard hit. But, people are always dying." Derreck's gaze swept across Nicole's face. Something dark lurked in his eyes, sending a chill coursing down to her toes. Or maybe she was being overly sensitive.

"I won't keep you any longer, Mr. Denner." Brett rapped his fist against the door frame. "One last question. Do you know anyone who has a red car?"

Something flickered at the corners of Derreck's eyes, but he seemed to catch himself. Or maybe she had imagined it.

"No. Why?" Derreck asked.

"They found red paint on the side of the vehicle Missy was driving. The witness claimed there were two cars on the road right before Missy drove into the lake. Perhaps this red car hit hers before she lost control." Brett directed his next question to Nicole. "Unless you can tell me your car had previous damage."

Nicole made an audible gasp. "No. My car didn't have any damage. So, are you saying a car *did* run Missy off the road?"

"Too early to say for sure. Someone may have collided with her and then left the scene of the accident. It happens. Sometimes if someone's drunk or on drugs, they make bad decisions." Brett's accusing gaze bore down on her.

"I'm sorry." The conversation flooded Nicole with horrible memories from her youth. A pool of sweat formed between her shoulder blades.

She took a step back. "I didn't mean to interrupt. I should go." Emotions—too many to articulate—crowded in on her. She needed to leave before she said or did something she'd regret.

"Wait, I'd like to talk to you." Brett caught her arm. "Can we talk over lunch?"

Derreck shuffled papers on his desk, pretending to be busy.

"I'm going to grab a bite in the break room. I have a lot of work to do."

"Come on." Brett tipped his head toward the door. "It'll be good to get away from work for a short break. That's okay with you, right, Derreck?"

Derreck peered over his glasses, seemingly uninterested. "Of course. Have a good lunch."

"Okay." Nicole hesitated, running her palm over her purse, wondering what she should do about the discrepancies in the documents. Her gut told her not to trust Derreck.

Her gut had been wrong before.

Brett held the door of the funeral home open for Nicole and watched as she wrapped her purple scarf around her neck and let the ends dangle down the front of her coat. The snow blew sideways on a stiff wind. She tugged on a matching knit cap that gave her a very youthful appearance. It reminded Brett of the waif of a girl who used to pull into his parents' driveway in some beat-up jalopy and beep, waiting for his younger brother, Max. Brett could never recall a time when she actually got out of the car and came to the front door.

Come to think of it, none of Max's friends came to the door.

Nicole stuck out her lower lip. "I'll never get used to this weather." She reached into her pocket and tugged on her mittens.

"They say cold weather builds character," Brett said. "I'm not sure who *they* are." The coffeehouse was only two blocks away from the funeral home. "You okay to walk? Or we could take my cruiser."

"Walking is fine." She eyed the police cruiser parked in front of the funeral home. "I don't want tongues wagging when they see me in that. It's taken me eight years to straighten out my life and it would only take one spin in the police car to ruin it."

"Let's walk, then."

They bowed their heads against the wind and plodded down the street. When they reached the bookstore, Nicole slowed, then gestured toward the door. "Let's go in here, instead." She grabbed the door handle with her bright pink mittens.

Brett followed. The bookstore owner, a balding gentleman with half-glasses perched on his nose, nodded to Brett and Nicole and went back to his coffee and reading material.

"Did you need a book?" Brett asked, uncertainty edging his tone. "I thought we'd get a sandwich at the coffeehouse."

"This is more private. I've maintained a low profile since I've been home. I don't want people to start talking about me now."

"Just because you're with me?"

"Precisely because I'm with you." She threw up her hands and turned on her heel toward the door. "Oh, this is crazy. I'm going back to work."

Brett grabbed her wrist and led her down an aisle of books, one side romance and the other suspense. The irony was not lost on him.

She spun around and held up a hand. The form of her mitten suggested she was pointing at him. He suppressed the urge to smile. The pointy mitten got very close to his face. She glared at him. "You can't tell me what to do."

He held up his hands in surrender. "I wouldn't dream of it." Brett gestured to the plush chairs in the back corner of the bookstore, completely private barring any back-of-the-store browsers. "Have a seat."

She arched a perfectly groomed eyebrow at him.

"Please?"

Nicole's features softened and warmth radiated through Brett's body. She eyed him and sat with a whoosh in her bulky winter coat. Patting the arms of the chair, she angled her head to look at him. She tugged off her mittens and unbuttoned her coat.

Brett took off his coat and tossed it on the footstool before sitting. Leaning forward, he rested his elbows on his thighs.

"I'm not the person you used to know." Nicole leaned back.

Brett jerked his head back, surprised by her candor.

She pointed at him. "You think I'm responsible for Missy's accident. Maybe we were partying and I handed over the keys to my car. That's what you think, right? That's why you asked me if she was under the influence. That's why you asked my boss if Missy was a good employee." Her voice had a desperate quality about it. "Or you're wondering if someone had a grudge against me and ran my car off the road, but instead of hurting me, they hurt Missy." Her eyebrow twitched as she seemed to fight back the harsh reality. Missy hadn't simply been hurt.

More than likely, Missy had been killed.

Brett threaded his fingers. "I'm investigating Missy's accident. That's all."

Nicole leaned forward. "I've changed. Please leave me alone." She started to push off the arms of the chair. Brett's hand on hers stopped her. Their gazes met and lingered.

"There was damage to your car." He watched her face carefully. Anger flashed in her eyes and then registered concern. "Someone wanted your car to go into the lake." He leaned in closer, nudging her knee with his. "*Your car.*"

Nicole leaned back and crossed her arms over her middle. "It doesn't make any sense." Worry settled into the corners of her eyes. "Isn't there a way the police can track down the make and model?" A sheepish expression flickered across her face. "I see it all the time on those detective shows."

Brett snorted and stopped short when Nicole didn't seem amused. "That takes time. Even when we do find the information, we have to find the specific car. Part of the investigation includes finding out if the victim—or the intended victim—had any enemies."

Nicole clutched her mittens in her hand. "You really think someone wanted to hurt me?" She let out a mirthless laugh. "I lead a pretty quiet life."

"You didn't always lead a quiet life."

Nicole narrowed her gaze at him.

"What about the drug dealer you testified against after my brother died?" Brett rarely talked about his brother. It was too painful. Even now. Brett blamed himself. He should have seen his brother was still using.

Her eyes flared wide. "He's in prison. He'll be there for a long time."

Brett made a mental note to check on the dealer's current status. "What about Missy, then? Did she complain of anyone harassing her? An old boyfriend?"

Nicole flattened her hand against her throat. "No, no. I can't see Missy having an enemy in her life. Everyone loved her." She stilled and all the color drained from her face. She bit her lip and regarded Brett, indecision in her eyes.

"Tell me. What is it?"

"Like I said the other day, she was going to visit a boyfriend in Buffalo. The thing is, I don't know anything about him." Nicole scratched her cheek and her speech halted. "I think she was dating someone in Silver Lake, too."

Excitement ramped up his pulse. "Do you know his name?"

Nicole slowly shook her head. "She said she couldn't

tell me. Something about it being too new. She didn't want to jinx it. Silly, really." She leaned forward and tugged off her coat and plucked at her shirt. "I think she thought I'd disapprove of this guy."

"Any ideas?"

Nicole shrugged. "None."

Brett ran his finger across his chin. "And you haven't had any run-ins with anyone lately?" A whisper of regret niggled at the back of his brain. He hadn't meant to say "lately" but it was hard not to think of his brother when it came to Nicole. She had been cast as the villain in Max's untimely death.

Was that fair?

"No I haven't had any run-ins." Sounding tired, she stood and swiped her coat from the chair. "This is exactly the reason I hate living in Silver Lake. You are all still judging me." Her eyes sparked with anger. "Do you ever wonder what *you* could have done to save your brother?"

Brett's stomach bottomed out. Of course he had. Brett thought he had guided his brother back onto the right path. But Nicole had had more influence. "You were with him that night. You could have stopped him."

She lifted her eyes to meet his. Her brows snapped together and her mouth opened, then closed as if she were about to say something, then changed her mind. "I'd give anything to change what happened that night. But I can't. I did the only thing I could. *I* changed."

Brett bit back an angry retort. His feelings were still raw when it came to his brother's untimely death.

Nicole planted her fist on her hip. "Now that you ask, I do have enemies. You and your family."

Her words cut to the core. "My family was devastated by Max's death."

Nicole drew in a deep breath and exhaled. "I don't think your mother or father would shed any tears if I ended up in the icy lake." Nicole's posture slumped and she pivoted toward the door.

"My parents were destroyed when Max died. But they're not heartless." Brett scrubbed his hand across his face.

Nicole slowly turned around, sympathy etched on her features. Brett had been so hurt by his brother's death, the only consideration he had given Nicole was blame.

Max had made his own mistakes. Since he was dead, Nicole was an easy target. Guilt twisted his insides.

Nicole bit her bottom lip. "I'll never get away from my past as long as I live in Silver Lake. I wish I lived somewhere where no one judges me for the stupid mistakes of my youth."

They locked eyes. She seemed to mentally shake her head. "I've got to get back to work."

Brett stepped into her path.

"What? Do you want to remind me of something else I did wrong?" Her tone held both impatience and annoyance.

"Do you have a good relationship with Ethan's father?" Brett found himself holding his breath, waiting for her answer. His pulse roared in his ears.

Splotches of red bloomed on her neck and cheeks. Nicole's wide-eyed gaze darted around the bookstore. "What does my son's father have to do with this?"

Brett never took his eyes from Nicole's face. "A woman's greatest enemy is often someone close to home."

Nicole stormed out of the bookstore. The bells clacked against the glass door, jarring her already frayed nerves. The wind whipped her face as a million thoughts assaulted her brain. She hated Silver Lake.

Hated, *hated* it.

Sometimes an obligation—like caring for her grandmother—trumped the strongest desire. Like the desire to move away.

Away from small-town gossips.

Away from the shameful mistakes of her past.

Away from Brett Eggert.

Ethan's father had nothing to do with this nightmare she was living. Ethan's father was dead.

Adjusting her scarf around her neck, she picked up her pace, determined to get back to the funeral home without discussing this mess with Brett anymore. She didn't want to answer any more questions, especially not about her son. She feared Brett had taken one look into her son's eyes and figured out Ethan was his nephew. Now he was using the investigation into Missy's accident to get answers.

It was none of his business. Ethan was *her* son. She had raised him alone for seven years. She had no plans to infect him with the poisonous venom the Eggert family would spew about her.

A throbbing started behind her eyes. She needed to quiet her mind or risk getting a migraine. She turned to prayer as she often did. *Oh, dear Lord, help me figure out how to deal with all this stress. I know I haven't always been the best person. But I'm trying. I'm trying so hard to move beyond the mistakes of my past. And please, please bring Missy home.*

"Hey, wait up," Brett hollered.

Nicole quickened her pace. She was done talking. The icy wind sucked the breath out of her.

Brett caught up with her. "Hold up."

She suspected most people froze at his commanding tone, but she wasn't most people. She bit back a snarky comment and forced a smile. A polite smile. The one reserved for limited interactions with the stone-throwing residents of Silver Lake, the smile that said, "I'll be pleasant, but I'll never like you."

Brett guided her closer to the building, out of the harsh winds. He surveyed the street, as if he cared what other people overheard.

Or saw.

Nicole's bubbling anger simmered with guilt over the choices she had made as a young woman. It didn't seem to matter how much she had changed, people still disliked her.

"I have to get to work." Nicole's cool tone was no match for the icy blast of air. "I can't lose this job."

"Who's Ethan's father?" Brett tilted his head, his eyes taking on a warmth that made her want to confess everything. But she couldn't. In a small town, a bad reputation clung to a person forever, like a bad hairstyle in the senior yearbook. Her son's grandparents—Brett's parents—might use their influence to gain access to their grandchild.

"None of your business." Nicole couldn't take that chance. She didn't want the Eggerts to fill her son's head with negative images of his mother…or worse. "And I can promise you, his father is not harassing me. So, move on with your investigation. Find Missy. Find who ran her off the road."

"Ethan was my brother's middle name." Brett searched her eyes with his gaze.

Nicole stepped back and bumped her heel against the wall. "Ethan's a popular name."

An ache throbbed behind her temples. What if the Eggerts wanted to take Ethan from her? Mr. Eggert was an influential lawyer. He'd use terms like "unfit mother," "unsuitable home environment," and "in the best interest of the child" to gain custody of her son.

`Gigi had tried to calm her worries. Courts always favored mothers.

Always?

The final image of her own mother pulling away from

Gigi's house had played over and over in her mind like the black moment in a Lifetime movie. Her mother had whispered in her ten-year-old daughter's ear that she'd be back for her. That she was the most important thing in her life. That the situation was only temporary.

Drugs proved too powerful. Nicole never saw her mother again.

Nicole had stumbled into drugs just like her mother. But Nicole cleaned up her act for her son because he was the most important thing in Nicole's life.

She blinked a few times, flipped her scarf over her shoulder and hiked up her chin. "I have a job and I'm running late."

Nicole spun on her heel and strode toward the funeral home. Her worries pelted her like the snowflakes blowing sideways. Head bowed, she picked up her pace, focusing all her energy on envisioning Missy running the vacuum in the front foyer when Nicole returned.

Please let Missy be okay.

"Nicole!" Brett's voice grew closer and held a hint of urgency that made her pulse spike. But she wasn't going to stop.

She broke into a jog. Apprehension and shame pressed heavy on her lungs. Why wouldn't this man leave her alone? She skirted around an elderly lady pushing a walker through the snowy sludge. She had to remain confident. Missy was going to be okay. God was a merciful God.

Then why can't you forgive yourself for Max's death?

Nicole slowed at the intersection and watched the blinking man count down five seconds. She could make it. She had to if she wanted to avoid Brett. She pulled her collar up and darted across the street. From the corner of her eye, she noticed a delivery truck bearing down on her. Tingles swept up her arms and her vision zeroed in on the safety of the sidewalk a few feet away. Her boot hit the curb. At the same time, slush sprayed the backs of her legs.

Just great. Annoyance tinged with relief made pools of sweat gather under her coat.

Nicole spun around to glare at the offending truck and she noticed Brett running toward her, the concern on his face making icy shards shoot through her veins. He wove around a compact car, slamming his hands on its hood just as it screeched to a halt, thankfully finding purchase on the plowed pavement. "What are you doing?" Nicole's heart jackhammered. She lifted shaky palms in a show of surrender. Brett had almost gotten run over. "Fine, I stopped. I'm not going anywhere. What do you want?"

Brett's firm gaze was fixed on something over her head. *Way* over her head. She was lifting her eyes to follow his gaze when Brett crashed into her, pushing her out of the way. He landed on top of her with an *oomph* on the hard, cold concrete. A chunk of ice smashed onto the sidewalk a foot from their tangled bodies.

THREE

"Oh, no." Nicole's two simple words were woefully inadequate for the terror seizing her heart. The weight of Brett's body covering hers made it difficult to fill her lungs.

"Are you okay?" Brett shifted his solid body from on top of hers and got to his feet. He clutched her wrist and helped her up, his attention focused warily above.

"I'm fine. I'm fine." Nicole blinked back the dizzying head rush from standing too quickly. Brett scanned the length of her, doubt and worry in his eyes.

He wrapped his arm around her shoulders and guided her—no, pushed her actually—toward the closest doorway. Nicole glanced over her shoulder to the top of the three-story, historic brick building. A row of icicles dangled from the overhang, a huge section missing from the corner.

"How did you know?" Nicole's teeth chattered, making it difficult to form the words.

"Someone's up there. I saw a person dressed in black on the roof, leaning over the side."

A melodic *ding-dong* chimed when they stepped into a shop. A mix of ammonia-based hair coloring and nail polish hit Nicole's nose just as nausea overwhelmed her.

Just her luck. Brett's idea of safety was EnVogue Salon, the only other place in town she could have practiced her craft—on people who were alive, that is. But she didn't want to cut hair in a hotbed of gossip where she'd be the target.

Nicole's stomach twisted. She pulled her coat around her like a protective shield. If only she had a hood. "The funeral home's only a block away," she whispered to Brett. "I'll hurry. I'll be fine." She clenched her jaw and drew in a deep breath. Who was she kidding with her act of bravery?

"Stay here." Brett's commanding tone sent adrenaline shooting through her veins. Did he really think she'd be hit by a second chunk of ice in one day? Tingling dread crept up her fingertips. Did he think she had been the target? That it hadn't been an accident? Perhaps someone was doing work on the roof. And it wasn't exactly unusual for icicles to fall from buildings in the middle of winter.

Two accidents in a matter of days. Missy's and hers. And Missy had been driving *her* car.

Nicole nodded and met his gaze. The intensity in his expression made her stomach hollow out.

Brett left and Nicole turned around. A handful of ladies—some with foils in their hair, others with cotton between their toes and all with slack-jawed expressions—peered out the window, chatting about the commotion that had just unfolded. The commotion where Nicole had been a central figure. Inwardly she groaned. This was her worst nightmare.

A tall woman in black pants and a white blouse with a plunging neckline stepped away from the window, scissors in her hand. Her waxed eyebrows pushing against a smooth forehead said more than any words. Nicole's face heated and she immediately felt eighteen again. And the target of all these small-town, small-minded, belittling women.

A petite, plump woman emerged from the crowd. Nicole's heart stopped.

Mrs. Eggert.

The older woman approached. She wore a black cape and had highlighting foils in her hair. "I heard you were in town." Her bored tone was meant to put Nicole in her place. Mrs. Eggert flicked her fingers toward the window as if she were shooing a bug away. "What was going on out there? Is my son okay?"

Nicole swallowed around a lump in her throat. "Brett... Chief Eggert is fine. He pushed me out of the way of an ice chunk." She hated the squeaky quality of her voice. For years, Nicole had imagined meeting Mrs. Eggert face-to-face—to finally have her say—and this wasn't exactly how it had unfolded in her mind.

Mrs. Eggert crossed her arms under her black plastic cape. "How gallant."

The other ladies drifted back to their chairs or workstations with ears finely tuned toward the conversation in the foyer.

"Brett asked me to stay here." Nicole tucked her fisted hands into her coat pockets for fear she'd bolt out the door. She angled her body away from the inquisitive eyes and fixed her gaze on the sidewalk outside. The unyielding cement had smashed the large icicles into glittery fragments.

If Brett hadn't intervened, her skull would not have fared as well.

Nicole drew her arms closer to her sides and stifled a shudder, not willing to reveal her vulnerability to these busybodies.

"I've never known you to listen to authority, dear." Mrs. Eggert returned to the stylist's chair and sat, as if upon a throne. Her words dripped with sugary disdain. The older woman's cool tone hung in the air, lingering around Nicole like a bad scent. She turned toward the door and watched the passing vehicles, hoping Brett would return soon.

A few minutes later, Brett stepped inside the small entryway, his masculinity out of place among rows of nail polish, a pedicure tub and the chatty ladies.

"Whoever it was, they're gone." Brett slipped his hand around Nicole's elbow to lead her closer to the door. "But they left this. I found it in the opposite corner of the roof behind a row of AC units." He held up a pickax. "Convenient for hacking off the icicles."

Nicole angled her head toward Brett and whispered, "And dropping them down on me?" She barely squeezed out the words through a too-tight throat.

"After your vehicle ended up in the lake, I'm not taking any chances." He shook his head and placed his hand on the salon door. "Let's get you safely home."

Nicole was about to protest, claiming she had to get back to work when a high-pitched voice sounded across the salon. "Is my son going to leave without saying hello to his mother?"

Brett spun around and fixed his gaze on his mother for the first time. "Sorry, Mother. I was distracted. I didn't see you here." He crossed the small space and planted a kiss on her cheek. "How's Father?"

His mother waved her hand. "Holed up in the carriage house working on that silly rowboat he'll never use. You know him. You need to come visit. It would do him good to see you."

"I will. Soon." Brett cleared his throat, clearly uncomfortable. "Sorry to run, but I have to see Nicole home."

Mrs. Eggert approached, her eyes and mouth pinched. "Stay away from my son." Her mouth twitched as if it took tremendous restraint not to say more.

"Mother. Please."

Brett's mother shifted her steely gaze to land on her only surviving son. "How can you stand this evil woman? It's her fault your brother's dead."

Nicole stumbled into the funeral home foyer, desperate to catch her breath. Desperate to be alone. She needed to reach deep inside and rely on her faith because her emotions—a tangle of shame, anger and grief—rioted within her and threatened to pull her under, sending her back to a dark time in her life.

She turned to slam the door closed and came up short. Brett planted his palm on the door. Contrition softened his rugged features. In no mood to be forgiving, she folded her arms across her chest and tipped her head. "Didn't you hear? I'm evil."

"My mother can't see past her grief." He stepped into the foyer and closed the door, shutting out the harsh winter elements.

Nicole slipped off her scarf and held up her hand. "No one in this town will ever see past the girl I used to be. I've made my peace with that. We don't have to pretend we're friends." She lowered her voice and pointed over her shoulder with her thumb. "I have work to do. So, please, let me do my job." Then she leaned closer. "While you're doing your job to see who might want me dead, check out your mother. She seems awfully unhappy I'm back in town."

Brett's mouth flattened into a thin line. "Forgiveness works both ways."

Nicole froze for a moment and gave him a pointed glare. Shaking her head, she yanked off her coat and grabbed a wire hanger, jamming it into her coat sleeves. Missy's pink jacket hanging on the rod taunted her.

"Would you put it past your mother to hire her gardener or someone else to kill…?" She couldn't finish the sentence. It was too ridiculous. Mrs. Eggert hire a hit man to kill her?

"Where did you put the pickax?"

"In my trunk. We'll see where it leads us."

Nicole dragged her hand across her head and pulled off her winter hat. "Please, just leave. I can't afford to lose this job." She dropped her shoulders in exasperation and a hint of capitulation. "I promise I'll be careful."

A thump and a shuffle drew her attention. Mr. Peters

made his way across the lobby, steadying himself with his cane. "Hello, Chief Eggert. Nicole. Seems there's a lot of commotion going on here."

Nicole shot Brett a please-don't-blow-this-for-me look. "Chief Eggert is investigating Missy's accident."

"Do you have news about Missy? We're terribly worried," Mr. Peters said, his voice exceptionally frail.

"I'm sorry, no."

Mr. Peters lifted his cane and gestured at Nicole's slush-covered leg. "Oh, my. What happened here?"

Nicole twisted to inspect the damage to her gray wool pants. "Me, a puddle and a delivery truck. Not a good combination."

"You need to change before you catch a cold." Mr. Peters tapped his cane on the carpet. "Let me find Gene. He can take you home. You shouldn't have to walk in this dreadful weather. Take the afternoon off. It's dead around here today." A faint smile stretched his thin lips, but didn't reach his eyes. Mr. Peters never seemed to grow tired of his dead-joke shtick, but today it fell flat.

"Oh, I don't need the afternoon off. I'll come back after I change. I can help at the wake."

Mr. Peters shook his head. "No, take the afternoon off. Mrs. Fenster is ready for the viewing this afternoon." He lowered his voice. "You did a beautiful job, dear. Her family will be pleased."

"I have some paperwork to do."

Mr. Peters shook his head. "No, you need a break. This whole Missy thing has rattled all of us."

Brett tugged on the scarf in Nicole's hand, leaving her no choice but to take a step closer to him. His warm gaze locked on hers. "I'll see that Nicole gets home safely."

Mr. Peters nodded slowly as if it were too painful to get out the words. "I'm going to go sit with my wife this afternoon. She likes when I bring home chocolate."

"That's nice." Nicole hesitated for a moment. "Are you okay? I know Missy has worked for you for a long time, both here and at your home." Nicole touched the sleeve of the older man's suit coat and felt a subtle tremble.

Mr. Peters took a few steps back and reached for the arm of a chair, lowering himself into it. Nicole wondered how much longer he'd be able to come in to work.

"I'm worried about Missy," Mr. Peters said, his voice thin and shaky. "So many things have been changing. I miss the simpler days." He placed one hand over the other on the curve of his cane. "Maybe it's time I finally retired. Derreck's ready to run things." The wrinkles around his lips grew more pronounced. "My wife needs me." Concern glistened in his eyes. "I haven't told Martha about Missy. She'll be devastated."

Words of comfort got lodged in Nicole's throat. She ran a hand along her purse strap, all too aware of the documents tucked inside. Was Derreck stealing from his uncle's funeral home?

Nicole tugged her scarf out of Brett's hand and stepped back, gaining courage. If she wanted people to treat her differently, she had to stand tall. Be courageous. Learn to trust. She surveyed the empty lobby. "Can we go into your office and talk, Mr. Peters?" She turned and strode to his office. "I need to tell you something I should have told you right from the start."

Brett and Mr. Peters followed her to the older gentleman's large office. Brett hung outside the door. "I'll let you have your privacy. Nicole, call me when you're ready to go home. I'll drive you."

Nicole cleared her throat. "If it's okay with you, Mr. Peters, I'd like Brett here. There have been too many strange things going on lately, I'm worried they're related."

Mr. Peters lifted a shaky hand, a nonplussed expression on his face. "If it makes you feel better."

Nicole closed the door and twisted her fingers together as she searched for the right words. She sat, then shifted to the edge of the seat while Brett hovered nearby. "I received a phone call from the King family a week or so ago."

Mr. Peters's chair creaked as he sat facing her. "We buried Abe King a few weeks ago. His son came up from Buffalo."

Nicole stopped fidgeting with her hands and folded them in her lap. "Yes, that's the one. Abe's son, Isaac, accused the funeral home of not providing the services his father had paid for when he made his prearrangements."

All the color drained from Mr. Peters's weathered face. "That can't be true." He pressed his palms on the glass surface of his desk and tried to stand, but slumped down in his large leather chair. "I'll pull his file. He won't find any discrepancies. I'm sure of it."

"I pulled the file. I had planned to meet with Mr. King, but canceled when my grandmother wasn't feeling well." And then she'd received the news about Missy's accident.

Mr. Peters leaned back. A vertical line creased the skin between his bushy eyebrows. "Why didn't you bring it to my attention immediately?"

Nicole sighed heavily. "I didn't want to worry you. You have a lot going on with Mrs. Peters. I thought I'd straighten things out with Mr. King and put this whole mess behind us." She lowered her eyes, then lifted them. "And I didn't want to jump to conclusions. I know what it's like to be at the receiving end of that." She gave Brett a cool stare.

"Jump to conclusions? Don't be silly." Mr. Peters ran a finger across his eyebrow. "Let's get to the bottom of this. You have the documentation?"

She nodded. "I have a fax." She pulled the papers out of

her purse and smoothed them across the desk. "Mr. King sent his father's copy."

Nicole flicked her gaze to Brett as he shifted his stance. Despite the hard feelings between them, Nicole was glad Brett was here. She wanted a witness that she had been trying to resolve the issue with the client and that she had not been a part of any possible deceit.

If it came to that.

Mr. Peters closed his eyes briefly and shook his head. He laughed quietly. "I wish you had come to me directly, dear. This happens often, I'm afraid."

Nicole bit her lower lip. "What do you mean?"

"A person makes funeral arrangements for himself. He gives his loved ones the paperwork. Then after time passes, he makes changes with us and fails to give the family updated paperwork. That's all this is."

Nicole pressed a hand to her chest. "I'm so relieved. Your nephew made the prearrangements. His signature was on the bottom. I thought…and there was another time I overheard a client arguing with Derreck in his office." She paused and drew a breath. "I'm sorry. I didn't know what to think."

Mr. Peters picked up a pen and tapped it on the desk, his thin lips tipping into a smile. "You thought Derreck was embezzling from the funeral home? Is that why you wanted Brett here?" His brittle laugh sent heat rising to her cheeks.

"I didn't know what to think." Doubt whispered across her brain. "I should have come directly to you."

Mr. Peters dropped the pen and slid the fax on top of the original document. "Don't worry about this. I'll contact the King family directly and clear this up. I appreciate your concerns, Nicole. But next time, when it comes to business-related things, don't hesitate to come directly to me or Derreck." He cleared his throat. "I trust Derreck as if he were my own son."

"I apologize," Nicole said, feeling the heat of Brett's gaze on her.

The older gentleman ran his knuckles across his chin. He seemed to mentally shake himself. "This is all part of doing business. People are upset, grief-stricken. They're often not thinking straight. It's a tough business we're in." He lifted his weathered hands. "No worries."

Brett tapped the back of her chair with his open palm. "While I have you both here, there's something else we should discuss."

Nicole shot him a dirty look. Mr. Peters had enough going on, but Brett wasn't deterred.

"Who has access to this building during the day?" Brett gestured to the front lobby.

Mr. Peters's eyebrows twitched as if he didn't understand. "We're a business. People can come and go as they please."

"I'm worried about Nicole's safety."

"I don't understand." Mr. Peters shuffled a few papers on his desk. "What's going on?"

Nicole huffed, not wanting to believe any of this. "Chief Eggert thinks that whoever ran my car off the road had been targeting me. That it wasn't an accident."

Mr. Peters scoffed. "The weather was bad. Poor Missy probably lost control. No one's to blame."

A fresh fist of grief squeezed her heart. Nicole blamed herself. At the very least, she should have convinced Missy to stay home considering the approaching winter storm. She could have said no when Missy asked to borrow the car.

"The car accident was one incident. A second one occurred only moments ago," Brett said, wrapping his hands around the back of her chair, his fingers brushing against her hair.

Mr. Peters slumped, looking genuinely ill. "What incident?"

Nicole threw up her hands, trying to act as if the event was no big deal, but icy fear knotted her stomach. "Ice fell from a building and nearly hit me. Ice falls off buildings all the time." She glared up at Brett.

Brett shook his head. "Or someone could have used the pickax I found on the roof to free the icicles as you were approaching."

Nicole threaded her hands through her hair. "This is all crazy." But deep in her heart, she knew Brett was right. Something strange was going on.

Mr. Peters shook his head. "It certainly sounds crazy. What do you need me to do, Chief Eggert?"

"Can you keep all the doors at the funeral home locked when Nicole is working?"

"But my business…" The elderly man's words trailed off as if he realized the seriousness of Brett's request.

"Perhaps you can put a note asking people to ring the doorbell," Brett suggested.

Mr. Peters shuffled the papers on the desk in front of him. "I can't very well inconvenience people at their time of grief. Can you imagine them coming to the funeral home only to find my door barricaded?" His gaze landed squarely on Nicole, concern and indecision dulling his blue eyes. "Maybe this would be a good time for you to take an extended vacation. I don't want anything to happen to you."

Nicole's heart sank and panic chugged through her veins. "I need this job."

"Your job will be here when you're ready to return." The lines deepened around Mr. Peters's eyes as he forced a conciliatory smile.

"Who will do the makeup? The paperwork?"

"Derreck and I are more than capable. Believe it or not, funeral directors can do hair and makeup. We just preferred to hire you." He ran his index finger across his chin, deep in thought. "My Martha used to do the makeup until she fell ill."

"I didn't know," Nicole muttered. She had only met the woman a few times before her health made her housebound. The elderly lady always struck Nicole as distant, maybe a little snooty. Nicole had a hard time imagining Mrs. Peters doing the deceased's makeup in the basement.

Mr. Peters pushed off the desktop and made it to his feet this time. "I need to spend some time with Martha. We enjoy having lunch together."

Nicole jumped to her feet. "You won't have to lock the front doors of the funeral home." She shot an accusatory gaze at Brett. *Stupid idea.* "I plan to be at work tomorrow morning."

Mr. Peters patted her shoulder as he walked around the front of his desk. "If you're sure." Something flitted across the elderly man's face that she couldn't quite identify. "I'd hate for anything to happen to you."

"It won't." She pushed back her shoulders.

They said their goodbyes and Brett led Nicole outside to his patrol car. She was too cold to refuse the ride. As he held open the car door for her, she spun around. "You almost cost me my job. I need this job. My family is counting on me. Unlike you, I don't come from money."

Brett narrowed his gaze and a chill pooled like an ice puddle in her gut. "You won't be able to help your family if you're dead."

"I see you've inherited your mother's flare for the dramatic." Nicole buckled her seat belt and stared straight ahead. If she had been a cartoon character, steam would have been spewing out her ears. "I'd appreciate it if you didn't try to get me fired."

"Someone ran *your* car off the road. Someone tried to drop a chuck of ice on *your* head. I'd hardly call that dramatic." He turned the key in the ignition. "That's reality."

A reality she didn't want to face.

A reality that made her testy.

Brett lowered his voice. "My job is to keep you safe."

"So far, so good." She shifted in her seat and stared out the passenger window. "Now if you could really do your job and find Missy, that would be just great." Nicole's sarcastic tone softened at the mention of her friend.

Brett's police radio crackled to life. A body had been found on the shores of Silver Lake. Nicole's heart plummeted as they locked gazes.

Brett jammed the gearshift into Drive. "I have to answer this call. I'll drop you home first."

"Take me with you. Please."

Indecision played across Brett's features. "You need to change your wet clothes."

"I need to see if they found Missy. *Please.*" Her pulse whooshed in her ears.

Brett gave her a slight nod, as if he understood the pain of not knowing. The engine roared at top speed. "When we get there, you're staying in the car. Hear me?" There was no mistaking the command in his tone.

"I hear you."

Brett parked along a curve in the road, a short distance from a steep incline dropping off to the lake. He was the first responder. He shifted in his seat, turned the heater on high and covered her cold hand with his. "Stay here. I'll be back as soon as I know anything."

Nicole nodded. She had a distant look in her eyes as she searched the horizon.

Brett pushed open the door and gave her one last warning. "Stay in the car."

He flipped up the collar on his jacket and carefully navigated down the snowy incline. A lone man and his dog stood at the edge of the lake. The dog reared up on his lead and the man patted its head reassuringly.

"What did you find?" No sooner had the words formed on Brett's cold lips than his gaze drifted to the edge of the lake. A form bobbed at the shoreline in a dark expanse of water not covered by ice. Long hair tangled in the tree roots pushing out into the cold lake waters. Brett turned to the man. "If you want to wait by the road, someone will get your statement shortly."

The man's somber expression reflected Brett's mood. Without saying a word, the older gentleman trudged up the incline, his dog barking forlornly as if realizing he was going to miss out on the action.

A second cruiser pulled up behind his and Ed Hanson joined him. "Oh, man," Ed groaned when he saw the body.

"Missy." Brett took careful steps along the edge of the lake. He bent and grabbed hold of the purple jacket and pulled the body to shore. Ed grabbed the other shoulder and together they flipped her over.

Cloudy, unseeing eyes stared up at them. His stomach clenched. *Missy Flowers.* He did a quick visual check of his vehicle and found Nicole had ignored his instructions. She stood on the road talking to the gentleman with the dog. Brett could only image what the man was saying, but at least Nicole couldn't see the body of her friend from her vantage point.

Brett tipped his head toward the other officer. "The coroner's here." The coroner, Suzanne Ernst, and her partner climbed out of their gray van and headed toward the lake. Brett squinted up at them. Suzanne was a petite woman with long blond hair pulled back into a tight ponytail. A navy knit cap covered her head.

"Is this the missing driver from the accident the other night?" Suzanne asked.

"Afraid so. Let's do what we can to preserve the scene, but it's going to be tough, considering the elements."

Suzanne nodded. Ed stood silent, a sentinel over the girl whose life had been snuffed out all too soon.

Brett watched Nicole, her back to him, as if trying to avoid the truth. A sick feeling seized his insides. "I need to tell Nicole."

Brett climbed the incline. Each carefully placed step seemed to take an eternity. When he finally reached Nicole, she spun around as if sensing him. The panic in her eyes said all he couldn't. Instinctively, he held out his arms and she fell into them. He ran a hand down her soft brown hair. "I'm sorry."

Nicole nodded against his chest. She sniffed and wiped her nose. She pulled away from him and met his gaze. Determination mixed with grief gave him pause. "May I see the…her?"

Near the shoreline, Suzanne and her assistant placed the body in a white body bag then hoisted it onto a red sled with Ed's help.

"Not a good idea."

"Please." She turned toward the lake, a resolute look in her eyes.

"Stay here. I don't want you to slip into the water. You can see her before they load her into the van."

Nicole seemed to wince at the reality of the situation.

Ed, Suzanne and her assistant guided the sled up the hill. When they reached the van, the assistant pulled out a gurney. Together they hoisted the bag onto it.

"Wait," Brett called to the coroner. He guided Nicole

by the small of her back. He sensed her quiet trembling. "Unzip the bag."

Suzanne's gaze shot from Brett to Nicole and back. Brett gave her a subtle nod. The coroner shrugged as if to say, "Your call."

The zipper slid past Missy's vacant eyes staring at the gunmetal sky, her purple lips, her bloated face. Nicole gasped and her fist flew to her mouth. Brett grabbed her firmly by the waist, steadying her. The coroner stopped when the zipper reached Missy's belt.

"She's wearing my jacket." Nicole's voice broke over a sob. Not taking her eyes off her friend, she muttered, "She was always borrowing my clothes. Now it seems silly that I let it bother me."

A flash of something hanging out of one of the jacket pockets caught Brett's eye. He slipped the plastic bag out of the pocket and fingered the contents. Jewelry. A few rings. Cuff links. A brooch.

A deep line marred Nicole's forehead.

"Did Missy own a lot of jewelry?"

All the color drained out of Nicole's face. "No," she whispered. "She was broke. That's why she borrowed my car."

The coroner zipped up the canvas bag. Brett handed the bag of jewelry to Ed. "Take this down to the station and catalog it. I have a feeling someone's going to be looking for this jewelry."

Brett tried to guide Nicole away from the coroner's van. "Come on, let's get you warmed up."

"The jewelry..." The words sounded slurred, her lips frozen from the cold.

"Do you know something about this, Nicole?"

"Yes."

"The jewelry was in your jacket. Is it yours? Your grandma's?"

Fire flashed in Nicole's brown eyes. "No, it's not mine." She lowered her eyes and drew in a deep breath.

"If you know something about this, you have to tell me. I can't help you if you don't tell me what's going on. You have to trust me." Confusion and frustration clouded his brain. "Someone is going to be looking for this."

Nicole shook her head. "No one's going to be looking for any of that jewelry. The owners are dead."

FOUR

Nicole was numb.

The drive home went by in a blur. Brett murmured words meant to be reassuring, but she couldn't focus. Missy was dead. All hopes that she'd return were dashed.

Brett pulled up her driveway. She didn't wait for him to come to a complete stop. She pulled the handle and jumped out of the car, gulping cold air into her lungs.

"Nicole—"

Poor, dead Missy.

Nausea welled up again. Nicole straightened and jogged up the walkway. Her foot slipped and her arms flailed out but she regained her balance. Grief and anger crushed her lungs, her soul, making it hard to breathe.

Missy's cold, dead eyes...

She'd never be able to scrub that horrible image out of her brain. Tears burned the back of her nose. She reached the front porch and spun around when she sensed Brett following her. "I need you to leave me alone."

"I'm not leaving until I know you're okay."

She tilted her head and studied his face. The compassion in his eyes was like a sucker punch to the gut. "You'd have to stay for a mighty long time. I lost a good friend today."

"I know. I'm sorry." Guilt creased the corners of his eyes. "I shouldn't have let you come with me. Can I come in, just for a minute? I'd feel better if I knew you had dry clothes, a little something to eat and I had a chance to talk to your family."

Her dark mood pushed in from all sides, making the small space on the porch seem very close. "I don't want you in my house. I don't want you to interrogate me about the jewelry. I already told you everything I know."

He raised an eyebrow. "You told me you didn't have anything to do with that jewelry, so what are you afraid of? Why are you pushing me away?"

"I came back to Silver Lake for my grandmother. I'm not interested in getting reacquainted with the Eggert family." She pulled out the key from her purse and inserted it into the lock. "You and your family would want nothing better than for me to leave town. Just like I did after your brother was…" She couldn't squeeze out the last word.

"You chose to leave." His tone sounded dark, ominous.

Nicole scoffed and pushed the door open. She spun around in the opening and leaned toward him and whispered, "I didn't have a choice. Your family made it miserable for me."

The Eggert family had been on a mission to make her life wretched. When she found out she was pregnant, she knew she had to leave. Get as far away from the Eggert family as possible. Ethan was all she had left and she wasn't about to let them get their hands on him.

"That's in the past." Brett held the storm door open, a hurt expression in his eyes.

"You're letting all the heat out." She planted a fist on her hip as if the heating bill was her top priority right now.

Brett tipped his head as if to say, "Really, that's what we're going to argue about?"

"You aren't going to leave until I let you in, are you?" She pulled off her knit cap and smoothed a hand over her hair.

He shook his head.

She held out her palm. "My grandmother always taught me to be gracious. And you did save me earlier today from the falling icicles." She forced the sarcasm, yet a chill skittered down her spine. What if he hadn't been around earlier? Nicole wouldn't be coming home tonight. She drew in a deep breath and let it out. "You can come in as long as you mention nothing—and I mean *nothing*—about what happened today. I don't want to worry Gigi. I'll tell her in my own time."

"Scout's honor." He held up his hand in what she suspected was a Boy Scout pledge of some kind. Humor lit his eyes and Nicole had an irrational urge to slug him.

Nicole begrudgingly stepped into the small foyer. Brett ran back to his car and pulled the keys out of the ignition, then rejoined her. Little feet padded across the hardwood floor. Nicole spun around and tiny prickles tickled the back of her neck. Had Ethan overheard them arguing?

Ethan's eyes opened wide. "Chief Eggert's here again!" He seemed to be yelling the announcement to his great-grandmother. A wave of relief washed over her. Her son was interested in the police officer who had come calling and not her careless rant.

Nicole held out her arm to pull her son into an embrace. Ethan planted a kiss on her cheek, his eyes never leaving Brett's face. She couldn't wait to crawl into bed tonight and read her son bedtime stories and forget everything that had happened today. She squeezed him a little tighter.

Missy. Her jacket. The stolen jewelry.

"Mom, I can't breathe," Ethan said, the way little kids do when they're annoyed.

Nicole released her grip and smoothed her hand down his shirt. "I'm glad to see my little man."

Brett held out his hand. Ethan shook it and puffed out his chest.

"Hello there, young man. Did you have a good day at school?"

Ethan turned up his nose. "I didn't get to be line leader.

Miss Gallivan picked Grace. I think she likes girls more than boys."

"That's not true," Nicole playfully scolded her son. "Weren't you line leader a couple of weeks ago?" Nicole hung her coat over the back of the chair in the kitchen.

"Maybe." Ethan seemed to deflate a little.

Nicole hooked her finger under his chin and forced him to meet her gaze. "Did you get in trouble today?"

Ethan lifted his shoulders and let them drop. He squirmed away from her. "Miss Gallivan always yells at me when *all* the kids are doing stuff."

"Ethan," Nicole admonished, "don't worry about anyone but yourself. You know how you're supposed to behave."

"Yes, Mom." Ethan dropped into a chair and Nicole felt a little guilty for scolding him in front of Brett.

Nicole tried to sound cheery. "I got a little wet today." The cold had permeated her bones and her head was beginning to pound. She wanted Brett to leave so she could take a shower, warm up and have some dinner, but he didn't seem in a hurry to go.

Gigi rolled her wheelchair in from the family room where she seemed to be spending more and more of her time. The television was her primary source of entertainment. Gigi's forehead crinkled when she noticed Nicole's wet clothing. "Get out of those wet clothes before you catch your death of a cold."

"I will."

Gigi flicked her fingers. "What are you waiting for? Go now. I'll handle everything out here."

"But…" Nicole's gaze bounced between her son and Brett. "I…"

"Go," her grandmother insisted.

"I'll be right back." Nicole lifted an eyebrow, a silent warning to Brett not to say anything about Missy.

"Ethan, perhaps you can offer our guest something to eat and drink."

Ethan's eyes brightened. "Okay." He jumped up, pulled open the fridge and started rattling off a list of refreshments. Nicole turned and jogged down the hall to the bathroom. The less time Brett spent with Ethan the better.

The next morning, Nicole woke up and for the briefest of moments all was well with the world. That was, until all the events of the past few days slithered into the conscious part of her brain, overwhelming her with grief, anger and confusion.

She got dressed, saw Ethan off to school and waited for the bus to the outskirts of town. Nicole had formulated a plan while she lay awake last night. When she felt overwhelmed, she had to act or her thoughts would consume her. She had decided to go directly to the Peterses' home to talk to her boss about the stolen jewelry. This way, they could have privacy. *Someone* who had access to the funeral home had stolen the jewelry. It wasn't her and she didn't want to believe it was Missy, either.

Seated on the bus, Nicole unbuttoned her coat and stuffed her pink mittens into her pockets. With scratchy eyes, she squinted out the steamed windows of the overheated bus. She tugged off her knit cap and clutched it in her lap. She had thought, when she purchased her Cube last fall, that her bus-riding days were over. However, until the insurance company paid her for her totaled car, her feet, the bus and the kindness of others were her primary sources of transportation.

She let her gaze blur, ignoring the few other riders getting on and off the bus in the center of town. Her thoughts drifted to Brett. Last night, after she changed into warm clothes and returned to the kitchen, he had said goodbye to Ethan abruptly and bailed. He'd told Ethan he had an emergency. However, as she kept replaying the evening, doubts crept in. Unease wiggled up her spine. Had something else made him leave?

While she was still in her bedroom, she had heard Ethan and Brett chatting and laughing. However, when she stepped into the kitchen, Brett's expression had been hard, accusatory. Did he know Ethan was his nephew? She had analyzed his departure a million times in her head as sleep eluded her until the wee hours of the morning.

Or had he decided she must have stolen the jewelry? It was a logical leap, even if it wasn't true. Nicole had access to the deceased's belongings and Missy had borrowed her jacket where the stolen items were found. This line of thinking fortified her decision to talk to Mr. Peters first thing this morning. To plead innocent.

Nicole shuddered at the thought of betraying the sacred trust families had placed in her and the other employees of Peters Funeral Home. She had made a lot of stupid decisions in her youth, but never in a million years would she consider stealing from anyone. *Ever.*

The diesel engine kicked in as the bus climbed the hill to stately homes in a mature neighborhood on the other side of town. Nicole pulled the cord and the bell dinged, alerting the bus driver to her stop. She smiled weakly at the driver and climbed down the steps. An ornate stone at the intersection aptly indicated a neighborhood called Hillside Estates.

Nicole tugged her knit cap back on, buttoned her coat and flipped up her collar. She found herself wishing she had worn her warmer ski jacket until the memory of Missy wearing that jacket in the body bag slammed into her brain. She strode up the road to a stately brick home with white pillars and an expansive front yard, currently buried in a good foot of snow. When she was a young girl, she had dreamed of living in a home like this.

As an adult she had given up on silly dreams.

Nicole swallowed hard. Her heart raced. She turned toward the street, second-guessing her decision to visit Mr. Peters at home. The tree branches swayed in the wind. No, she had come this far. She couldn't chicken out now. She climbed the steps and rang the doorbell. The chime was some familiar melody reminiscent of elevator music. Nervousness swirled in her stomach.

Lord, please help me find the right words to make this right with Mr. Peters.

Mr. Peters had always been kind to her. Given her a job when jobs were hard to come by. He'd know she had nothing to do with the jewelry they found on Missy.

In her jacket. Her stomach lurched.

Nicole pressed a hand to her midsection. She turned to face the street. A young woman was speed-walking on the road, her hands pumping at her sides. Nicole watched the woman disappear around the corner.

Nicole sighed heavily. What was she thinking coming here? The door flew open and she turned back around.

Too late.

A flash of confusion lit Mr. Peters's eyes. He quickly recovered and motioned her in. "My, what are you doing here?" He patted her on the shoulder as she stepped up onto the marble foyer. "I heard they found Missy. I'm so sorry. She was a sweet girl." He paused and shook his head. "Such a tragedy."

"I...uh..." The need to plead her case suddenly seemed silly in light of Missy's death. "I'm sorry to bother you at home, but..."

"Dear, who is it?" A frail voice sounded from the intercom inside the foyer.

Mr. Peters turned and shuffled over to the intercom. "It's Nicole Braun, dear."

"Don't leave her standing at the door." Mrs. Peters's voice crackled over the speaker. "Bring her in."

Mr. Peters tilted his head. "Come in. Mrs. Peters will be happy for the company. She doesn't have much nowadays. Missy used to come by to clean." He made a pained sound deep in his throat. "Now it's mostly just the nurse and Gene. She has poor Gene running all her errands." He shook his head as he closed the door. Then, as if suddenly remembering something he lifted a gnarled finger. "Oh, and my nephew likes to visit now and again." He lowered his voice conspiratorially. "He comes by to make sure he stays in my wife's good graces." His eyes met hers. "She'll be happy to see a new face." Something in his flat tone gave her doubts.

Nicole smiled and followed her boss across the marble floor through the kitchen to a sunroom with floor-to-ceiling windows in the back of the house.

"Good morning, Mrs. Peters, I'm sorry to bother you…" Suddenly Nicole's misgivings formed a knot in her throat and her fight-or-flight responses kicked into overdrive. Flight was winning.

Mrs. Peters reclined in a chaise lounge next to windows that overlooked a large treed lot. She appeared exceptionally frail in a silk robe. A thick gray blanket covered her thin legs. The wall-mounted intercom was within easy reach. "My husband didn't tell me you were coming—" she paused to catch her breath "—or I would have gotten dressed."

Nicole held up her hand to protest and smiled sheepishly at her one pink mitten. She shoved it into her pocket with the other one. "I'm afraid my grandmother would think my manners were atrocious. I should have called first."

Mrs. Peters fumbled with the teacup on the table by her chair. It clattered against the saucer. She never lifted it to her lips.

"I'll help you, dear." Mr. Peters walked across the room using his cane, his free hand extended as if to grab the teacup and offer his wife a sip.

Mrs. Peters lifted an empty, shaky hand on an unbelievably thin arm. "I'm perfectly fine." Nicole realized Mrs. Peters's tone was meant to admonish, but its thin quality was less than convincing.

Nicole stuffed her hand in her pocket and fingered the knit fabric of her mitten. "I'm sorry to disturb you."

"You may as well sit since you're here." Mrs. Peters coughed. "Shame about Missy. We'll miss her around here. She kept this place spotless. I certainly can't clean anymore."

Nicole nodded and sat on the edge of a formal couch, its red fabric faded from the sun. Nicole should have considered the possibility of having this conversation in front of Mrs. Peters. She had mistakenly assumed the elderly woman would have been bedridden upstairs. Nicole didn't have much choice now. Mrs. Peters had been friendly with her grandmother in her youth. Maybe that counted for something.

Mr. Peters shuffled over and wrapped his gnarled fingers around the back of a chair with ornate wood carvings. "What can I do for you? Did you change your mind about taking some time off?"

"I'd rather keep busy, if that's okay."

Mr. Peters gave her a quick nod.

Nicole studied the intricate carvings. "I don't know where to start."

"Try at the beginning," Mrs. Peters said, her tone frank.

"I imagine you talked to Chief Eggert."

Mr. Peters's thick brows twitched. He seemed to consider something, then recover. "We'll be taking care of Missy's arrangements. Is that why you're here? No need to worry."

"Thank you, I'm sure her mother will appreciate that." Guilt nudged her. Nicole should have put aside her own grief and called Mrs. Flowers. "Chief Eggert didn't tell you anything else?" Nicole felt like a kid again, trying to figure out how much her grandmother knew so Nicole could decide how much trouble she was in.

Mr. Peters shuffled his feet and adjusted his grip around the back of the chair. "You're not going to keep me guessing, are you?"

Heat swept up Nicole's cheeks. She undid the buttons on her coat and pushed it off her shoulders, letting the coat pool behind her on the couch. Nervously, she pulled a mitten out of her pocket and flattened it on her thigh and tried to think how an innocent person would act.

Squared shoulders.

Eye contact.

Calm tone.

Plead your case. You are not a scared teenager.

And you are *innocent.*

"You gave me a job when I needed one and I would never do anything to jeopardize it." Nicole ran her hand along the mitten's hand-stitched seams.

"Of course. Did something happen?" Mr. Peters walked around to the front of the chair and sat. He hooked his cane on its arm.

Nicole felt breathless. She studied Mr. Peters's face. He seemed more frail than usual. "When they found Missy's body, she was wearing my jacket. She often borrowed my stuff without asking." No, wait, that didn't sound right. She couldn't blame her friend. Nicole cleared her throat. "I mean…"

Mrs. Peters's teacup rattled in the saucer and her lips gathered into a wrinkled bud.

"When they found Missy…" Nicole's throat closed

around a fist of grief. "They found jewelry in her pockets. The pockets of my jacket."

Mr. Peters ran a shaky hand over his brow and narrowed his gaze. "Jewelry in the pockets?" If Nicole hadn't seen it herself she wouldn't believe a pale man could grow even paler. "Where did the jewelry come from? Please don't tell me…"

Nicole ran her palms down her thighs. "Yes, it's jewelry from clients at the funeral home."

Mr. Peters wrapped his hands around the crook of his cane and pulled himself to a standing position. "How can that be?" Disbelief edged his tone. He slowly lifted his eyes. "Missy stole from us?"

"Oh, no, no. Missy would never have stolen from the funeral home. It makes no sense. Missy never had access to the bodies. She ran a vacuum. She dusted. She worked on the main floor of the funeral home." A throbbing started behind her eyes. A hint of doubt whispered across her brain. "I didn't come here to accuse Missy of anything. I came here to assure you I had nothing to do with it."

"Are you afraid you'll be accused in light of your past?" Mrs. Peters smoothed a wrinkled hand down the plush blanket covering her legs. Her voice sounded strong, assured.

Nicole nodded. "Honestly, yes. You might think my past is a predictor of future behavior." She wrung her hands. She was babbling, repeating things her therapist or maybe Dr. Phil might have said. Their jargon got intertwined after a while. "I wanted you to know I would never steal from you or anyone. I hope when Chief Eggert talks to you, you'll tell him I've been a loyal employee." The words rang hollow in her ears. She was a loyal employee, but it seemed fruitless when she had to tell someone else what to say when they vouched for her.

Mrs. Peters pressed a crumbled tissue to her lips. "How

did the jewelry get into your pocket?" She pointed a shaky finger at Nicole. "The pocket of *your* jacket?"

Mr. Peters's face flushed with color.

Nicole pushed her shoulders back. She needed to act confident. Innocent. "I don't know."

"And you expect us to buy your story?" Mrs. Peters squeezed fistfuls of the blanket.

Nicole was taken aback by Mrs. Peters's stern rebuke. "It's the truth."

Mrs. Peters's lips twitched. "*My* grandfather started the funeral home over a hundred years ago. When my husband took over the business, he changed the name to Peters Funeral Home." She stared wistfully into the distance as if a long-ago memory was playing in her mind. "The things we do for love."

Nicole glanced at Mr. Peters who seemed lost in thoughts of his own.

"Long before that," Mrs. Peters continued, "the funeral home had been in my family name. *We've* always prided ourselves on client trust. If word gets out that an employee has been stealing from our clients…" She paused and collapsed into a coughing fit.

"I promise you, I've never stolen anything from the funeral home." Nicole twisted her hands in her lap and her cheeks burned. She realized how odd her statement sounded. "When I was a teenager, I got into trouble. I'm not the same person." She pleaded with Mr. Peters. "I would never do anything to betray your trust."

Mrs. Peters hiked her narrow chin. Mr. Peters crossed his arm over his chest. "Perhaps it would be best if you *did* take some time off."

"What? Doesn't it mean anything that I came to your home to talk to you myself to clear my name?"

"A thief is bad for business." The older woman lifted

a shaky hand to her mouth and coughed into a wrinkled napkin.

"I am not a thief."

Mrs. Peters gave her a pointed glare. "Even a whiff of impropriety is too much."

"I'm not the same person who left Silver Lake eight years ago." Nicole's pulse beat wildly in her ears. All the work she had done to overcome her reputation was unraveling right in front of her.

Mr. Peters cleared his throat. He touched his wife's foot through the thick blanket. "Maybe we're being too rash. Nicole has never given me reason to speculate…"

"You never had a stomach for business." Mrs. Peters ran pinched fingers along the edge of the blanket. "My father would have never put up with disloyal employees. Or my grandfather."

Mr. Peters straightened as if someone had slipped a rod into his backbone. "Take some time off, Nicole. A little vacation." He softened his tone. "Grieve for your friend. We'll get to the bottom of this."

The walls pushed in on Nicole and the room began to swirl. She feared she'd pass out. "I need this job."

Worry lined Mr. Peters's eyes, but Mrs. Peters, despite her frail state, held her ground. "There are consequences for our behavior."

Nicole stood and grabbed the arm of the sofa to steady herself. "I promise you, Mr. and Mrs. Peters, I did not steal the jewelry they found in the jacket that Missy was wearing."

Mrs. Peters took a moment to recover from another coughing jag. "Was your friend Missy a thief?"

"No," Nicole blurted out. "Missy was not a thief." Nicole would never speak poorly about her friend.

Mrs. Peters raised an eyebrow. "So, then, who stole the jewelry?"

"I'm confident Chief Eggert will find the true thief." Nicole draped her coat over her arm and Mr. Peters ushered her to the front door. "May I please collect my personal belongings from the funeral home before my *vacation*?" Nicole couldn't keep the disdain from her voice.

"Of course, of course," Mr. Peters said in hushed tones, glancing toward the sunroom. When they reached the door, Mr. Peters leaned in close. "My wife is frail, but I have to respect her wishes." He opened the door and Nicole stepped out into the cool frigid air and gulped in big breaths.

Gene Gentry offered Brett a seat in Derreck's office with minimal discussion and left him there. Brett imagined the guy had found his calling working with the deceased. Mr. Peters wasn't in the office yet, so Brett had no choice but to discuss the jewelry situation with Mrs. Peters's nephew.

Brett took off his hat and tossed it on the adjacent chair. He blinked, his eyes felt gritty. He had hardly slept last night. He was convinced now more than ever that Ethan was his brother's son. *His nephew.* He needed to confront Nicole and ask her why she had kept this secret from him.

Anger fisted in his gut. His family deserved to know Ethan.

A little voice in the back of his head gave him the answer he wasn't willing to examine in the light of day. His family hadn't exactly given Nicole reason to engage with them after Max's horrific accident. They had made her life miserable. His father the hotshot lawyer had promised to ruin her if she so much as got a parking ticket in Silver Lake.

His father was a different man now. Illness could do that to a man. But his mother was as angry as ever. Eight years was a long time to carry such burdens.

It was time to face Nicole. Get her to admit Ethan was his nephew. Try to bridge the gap between their families.

Brett shifted in his seat and checked his phone discreetly. His patience wore thin as he waited for Derreck at the funeral home. He unbuttoned his coat. The temperature in the small office was a little too toasty for him. He touched the pocket that held the stolen jewelry. How had this jewelry gotten into Nicole's jacket pocket? Rubbing a hand across the back of his neck, he didn't want to consider the possibility that she had taken the jewelry off the bodies before burial. The act seemed contrary to the woman he was getting to know.

She's a no-good loser who dragged our son down with her. His father's angry words from nearly a decade ago scraped across his brain.

Brett shook the thought away. He wasn't as cynical as his father had been and he wanted to believe the best of people, including Nicole. He just hoped she didn't prove him wrong.

"To what do I owe yet another visit from our chief of police?" Derreck's booming voice shattered Brett's wandering thoughts.

Brett stood and shook Derreck's hand. "Thanks for meeting with me."

Derreck held out his hand, indicating the chair. Brett sat back down and Derreck took his place behind the large desk. "Shame about Missy. Did you figure out who ran her off the road?"

Brett eyed him suspiciously. "We haven't determined conclusively that she was run off the road."

Derreck lifted his palms. "My mistake." He chewed on his thumbnail for a second, before removing it from his mouth. "Is there something I can help you with?"

Brett reached into his pocket and pulled out the bag of jewelry. He tossed it on Derreck's paper-littered desk.

It landed with a tinny thud, the sound of metal clanking against metal.

A line creased Derreck's forehead. "What's this?"

"You don't recognize these pieces?"

"Should I?"

"You're not directly involved with preparation of the bodies?"

Derreck folded his hands on the desk in front of him, but didn't touch the bag, as if its contents could burn him. Or incriminate him. "Are you saying this jewelry belongs to the deceased?"

"Yes." Brett leaned forward. "Any idea who may have stolen these pieces?"

Derreck inspected the bag briefly. The overhead light reflected off the lenses of his glasses, obscuring his eyes. "Where did you find this?"

Brett let out a sigh. "I'd rather not say. Have you had any problems in the past at the funeral home? Things going missing?"

Derreck pulled out a white handkerchief and mopped his forehead. "Does this have anything to do with Missy's accident?"

An alarm clamored in Brett's head. "Why would you say that?"

"I may just run a funeral home, but I'm not stupid. You found this in Missy's possession, didn't you?"

Derreck took Brett's silence as agreement. "Strange, because it's not Missy I'd suspect of stealing." He wagged his index finger. "Now Nicole, I wouldn't trust her as far as I could throw her. That girl is troubled. But my uncle is an old softy. Can't say no to a lost cause."

"What makes you think Nicole stole the jewelry?" A throbbing started behind Brett's eyes. His gut told him Nicole was innocent, but he had to gather the facts.

A smirk flashed across Derreck's face and disappeared.

If Brett hadn't been watching Derreck, he'd have missed it. "I didn't think I needed to tell you."

A muscle ticked in Brett's jaw.

"Wasn't she the one all messed up with drugs when your brother died?"

Brett cleared his throat, trying to quell his emotions. "She's changed." Brett didn't know if he was trying to convince Derreck or himself.

"If you say so." Derreck leaned back and clasped his hands behind his neck, a smug expression on his face.

"If that's how you feel, why is she employed here?"

"Like I said, the old man is soft. Nicole needed a job, we needed a cosmetologist." He hiked an eyebrow.

"Seems to me, if you didn't trust Nicole, you would have insisted your uncle didn't hire her."

"My uncle's old. He'll retire soon." Derreck dropped his arms and leaned forward. "I'll be in charge soon enough. But, in all honesty, how many people want to work with the dead? Nicole's good at her job. There are trade-offs when you run a business. I just hate to think she resorted to stealing."

"We don't know that she has." Brett ran a hand across his mouth. "We need to make arrangements to return the jewelry to its rightful owners."

"I suspect the rightful owners are six feet under."

"Then their families." Brett sighed, growing weary of this discussion. "Do you have records of the jewelry?"

"We should have notes in the files. We can go back through and try to match up the pieces." Derreck scratched his forehead. "Strange, though, a family member usually watches the casket as it's closed to serve as a witness that the jewelry is still on the deceased and will be buried with them." He held out his hand to the bag on his desk. "This should have never happened."

"Who has access to the deceased?"

"The bodies?" Derreck seemed to be giving it some thought. "Nicole—" he lifted his face as if his glasses were too heavy for his nose and he ticked the names off on his fingers "—Gene, myself, my uncle." He shrugged. "Missy, I suppose, if she wandered down to the basement, but her job was to clean the upstairs. She didn't have business in the basement." His eyes narrowed as if he was reconsidering. "She may have had access when the bodies were in the viewing room, but she would have been taking a huge chance. My uncle and I have offices right across the hall." He drummed his fingers on the glass surface of his desk. "Actually, anyone could have wandered into the basement. We sometimes prop open the side door when we have flower deliveries." Derreck shrugged, acknowledging he had opened up the pool of suspects, but nothing changed the fact that the jewelry was found on Missy's body.

Brett reached out and scooped up the jewelry. "After my department catalogs the jewelry, I'll give you the photos to use to match everything with the deceased."

"This is going to be a nightmare. Horrible for business."

"The jewelry has to be returned."

The floor creaked as Derreck tipped back. "Business is tough as it is."

"You're the only funeral home in town."

Derreck laughed. "People are more than willing to drive forty-five minutes to Buffalo if they think we're robbing their loved ones." He dragged a hand through his thinning hair. "We're a small-town funeral home. Our population is limited, as it is."

"I'm not in the business of damage control. You're on your own for that one." Brett thought of Nicole, her son and grandmother living in that small house. She couldn't afford to lose her job. But that wasn't his problem, was it?

As if reading his mind, Derreck said, "I can't rightfully

fire Nicole without proof that she's the one who stole the jewelry, now can I?"

"I never said Nicole stole the jewelry."

"But you haven't ruled her out?"

"You just told me yourself a lot of people have access to the bodies." Brett turned and stepped into the hall, nearly slamming into Nicole.

Nicole shook her head in disgust and leaned in close. "Thanks for the vote of confidence."

"I have to do a thorough investigation."

Nicole tapped his chest with her closed fist. "For once, go with your heart. Does your heart say I'm guilty?"

No.

His heart also told him he'd fall for this feisty brunette if he wasn't careful.

FIVE

Something flashed in Brett's eyes that made Nicole's anger dissipate and sent warmth coiling around her heart. Was he humoring her or...?

Oh, no.

The last thing she needed was a romantic complication with the chief of police when she was suspected of stealing from the dead.

"I'm going to get to the bottom of this." He brushed his hand down her coat sleeve.

Not exactly a ringing endorsement of her innocence.

Nicole stepped toward Derreck's office so he could be part of this conversation. "I'm innocent." She enunciated each word for emphasis. "I did not steal the jewelry and neither did Missy. She wasn't that kind of person." Her pulse beat wildly in her ears.

"Years ago, when I stupidly got into trouble, I didn't stick up for myself. I'm not that same girl. I can't stay silent anymore." She hiked her chin, feigning confidence. Years ago, her silence had only gotten her accused of far more egregious things than she'd ever dream of doing. Guilt had made her feel as if she deserved whatever she had coming to her.

No more. Now she had a son to consider. She couldn't run away anytime things got difficult.

"Are you saying you had nothing to do with—" Derreck's gaze flicked to Brett and the mortician's lips thinned into a grimace "—with Max's death?"

"Leave my brother out of this." Brett gritted his teeth, his pain evident.

Nicole had a hard time catching her breath.

Brett rested his hand on the small of her back. "Nicole, we'll figure this out." She couldn't decide if she could trust him, but she realized she didn't have much of a choice.

"Perhaps your uncle was too quick to dismiss the discrepancies in the invoices." The words poured from her mouth before she had a chance to call them back.

Derreck jerked his head back. "You're still harping on that? My uncle told me about your concerns. My uncle also explained that any discrepancies on the contracts were a misunderstanding."

Brett put his hand on Nicole's forearm, but the torrent of words couldn't be contained.

"That's a convenient excuse. What would stop you from cheating clients?" She held up her hand, her index finger and thumb an inch apart. "Just a little bit. But enough to buy your new car or put a down payment on a new house."

"You are mistaken." Derreck's face was a perfect mask of denial, making Nicole doubt her accusations. Maybe Mr. Peters was right. Maybe the client was mistaken, but in her rush to put Derreck in his place, she'd lost sight of that.

Nicole crossed her arms to steel herself against her sudden doubts and embarrassment. She had no right to lash out at Derreck. Mr. Peters had explained away the discrepancies.

Derreck laughed. "People often ask questions regarding the contracts. Often the deceased make the plans, but their loved ones are left to finalize those plans." He held up his palms. "It only makes sense." He shook his head in obvious disgust. "Yet, you're going to stand here in front of the chief of police and accuse me of embezzling money from the funeral home?" Derreck's eyes narrowed into angry slits.

A fire burned in Nicole's gut. "I'm sorry. I shouldn't have said anything."

Derreck's dark gaze penetrated through her and an unsettling feeling swept over her. "How convenient that you bring this up now. All things considered."

Nicole rubbed her temples. A headache throbbed behind her eyes. "It doesn't matter anymore. The Peters have asked me to take a *vacation* until all this blows over."

A smug smile spread across Derreck's round face. "My uncle does have a backbone."

Brett flinched. "I'm sorry."

Derreck leaned forward and rested his elbows on the desk. "My uncle should have consulted me. This decision affects both of us."

"Would your decision have been any different?" Surprise laced her tone.

A harsh laugh scraped across her nerves. "I can tell you one thing, with you on vacation, I'm going to have to do the extra paperwork and makeup and hair. I can handle the paperwork. I'm not a fan of the other, even though most funeral directors do hair and makeup on a regular basis."

Derreck's eyebrows snapped together as if he had just thought of something. "When did you talk to my uncle?"

"This morning. I took the bus to their home. I thought I could convince him of my innocence."

"I'm surprised he's making you take a vacation," Derreck said. "He always speaks highly of you."

"Your aunt had other ideas."

Derreck nodded, understanding dawning on his features. "Makes sense. My aunt may be in frail health, but she's as feisty as ever. Never underestimate Aunt Martha. My uncle's no dummy. If Aunt Martha wants something, she gets it. No one makes a fool of her. If she thinks for a minute you had something to do with these thefts, she'll be your worst enemy. The funeral home is our family's legacy."

Nicole's stomach flipped. This day had gone from bad to worse.

The chime on the front door sounded. Nicole stepped into the hall to see a woman enter the funeral home's foyer and stomp the snow from her boots. She pushed back her hood and searched the lobby with a lost, forlorn expression as if she wasn't sure she was in the right place. Nicole had witnessed this emotion on countless faces of the bereaved.

Nicole stepped forward to greet her, then remembered she was technically on vacation. Nicole couldn't allow herself to be rude on account of semantics. This woman was obviously in pain.

"Hello, can I help you?" Nicole asked.

The woman's almond-shaped eyes were so utterly familiar that all the air whooshed from Nicole's lungs. "Mrs. Flowers?"

The woman's eyes widened in shock. "Yes. I'm here…" the woman's voice shook "…to make funeral arrangements for my daughter, Missy."

"Please, come into my office." Derreck had joined them, smoothing a hand down his gray tie, a touch lighter than his gray suit.

The woman nodded and took a step toward the office. Nicole put her hand on her forearm, stopping her. "Missy and I were good friends. My name is Nicole."

The woman lifted her watery eyes and a quivering smile strained her lips. "Oh, she spoke of you. You were a good friend to her." Missy's mother made it sound like an apology.

"You strongly resemble her." It was almost eerie. Nicole laughed nervously. "I guess it would be more appropriate for me to say she resembled you."

The comment infused levity into the room and Mrs. Flowers smiled. "Yes, she did." She swiped a tissue under her nose. "I haven't seen her in a while. I'm afraid we let time and distance get between us." A strangled sob escaped her lips. She fisted her hand and pressed it to her mouth. "Can you help me with the funeral arrangements?"

Nicole shot a sideways glance at Derreck. Brett had moved toward the door, as if to leave. Nicole had only been here to collect her belongings before her forced vacation.

Derreck gave her a subtle nod. "I'll sit down and go through everything with you," he said, "but I'm sure Nicole can join us."

Missy's mother smiled tightly at her. "I would like that."

A shaky breath squeezed from Nicole's lungs. How could she ever help this dear woman plan a funeral for her daughter, for *her* dear friend?

"Mrs. Flowers, I'm Chief Eggert." He held out his hand and the woman hesitated.

"We spoke on the phone." Mrs. Flowers's tone softened. "Thank you for keeping me informed regarding the investigation. It means a lot." The older woman dropped her arms to her sides, then she clutched her hands in front of her. "Do you have any new information about my daughter's…accident?"

"Not yet," Brett said, "but I promise we're still investigating."

"Thank you."

"I'll be on my way." Brett put his hat on, tipped it toward Mrs. Flowers and turned to Nicole. "Call me when you're finished. I'll drive you home."

Nicole opened her mouth to refuse his ride. Then she met his determined gaze. Her refusal died on her lips. "I'll call you when I'm ready."

"Oh, dear, I didn't mean to keep you from your plans," Mrs. Flowers said.

Nicole reached out and covered the woman's clenched hands. Guilt nudged Nicole. She didn't have any concrete evidence, but she knew with all her heart this poor sweet mother lost her daughter because of her.

Gloria Flowers's grip scrunched Nicole's knuckles. "I don't know how I'm going to get through this. She was my daughter. My only child."

"I'm so sorry," Nicole said for what seemed to be the hundredth time. Her throat ached from pent-up grief. Her words felt hollow. What else could she say?

Missy wouldn't be dead if she hadn't borrowed my car.

Nicole provided emotional support and Derreck filled out the paperwork and gave Missy's mother all the information regarding services and costs. Nicole suspected Mr. Peters would take care of the latter. Derreck excused himself to make a phone call and left them in his office.

"Would you like me to pick something for her to wear?" An emptiness spread and hollowed out Nicole's stomach.

Mrs. Flowers bowed her head and covered her face with her hands. "I don't know how I'd choose. I don't even know what she liked. She was so stubborn. We butted heads on everything. Now she's gone."

Nicole flattened her cool palm on her throat. "This may sound strange, but Missy loved a pink cable-knit sweater I own. Perhaps we could…" The word *bury* got lodged in her throat. "Perhaps she could wear my pink sweater."

Mrs. Flowers lifted her head; grief haunted her eyes. Slowly, a sad smile trembled on her thin lips. "Thank you."

"It would be my honor to do Missy's hair and makeup." Nicole scooted to the front of her chair to face the woman.

Mrs. Flowers blew her nose. "I could never afford to take Missy to have her hair and makeup done. Now…" She squared her shoulders and closed her eyes, clearly trying mightily to hold back another crying jag.

"I'll make sure she's taken care of." Even if Nicole had to go against Mrs. Peters's wishes and postpone her forced vacation, she had to do this one last thing for her friend.

Nicole's cell phone rang. Instinctively, her eyes darted to the clock on the wall behind Derreck's desk. Her heart plummeted.

Ethan.

Holding her breath, she answered the phone. "Hello."

"Mrs. Braun?"

Ms. But she decided now was not the time to correct the person on the other end of the phone. "Yes."

"This is Mrs. Finnen in the main office of Silver Lake Elementary."

Nicole swallowed hard. "Is everything okay?"

"Yes, Ethan's fine, but he missed the bus."

"Excuse me? How did this happen?"

An unmistakably weary sigh sounded over the phone line. "We need you to come get your son. The office closes in ten minutes."

Nicole turned her back to her friend's grieving mother and dragged a hand through her hair. She mentally calculated the time it would take to walk to the school or catch a bus and she feared Ethan would be waiting out in front of the school.

She highly doubted the school would leave him alone. But then she'd have to live with the stigma of being the mother who couldn't collect her child promptly from school when the office called. Nicole did not want to be the object of any more gossip.

If that were possible.

She swiveled on the edge of her seat. Mrs. Flowers stared at a wallet-sized photo of Missy cupped in her palm.

Determination settled over Nicole.

Into the phone she said, "Please tell my son Chief Eggert will pick him up. Do you know Chief Eggert?"

"Yes," the woman on the other end of the line muttered, a trace of indignation in her tone.

"Well, I am giving Chief Eggert authority to pick up my son. Please tell my son." She ended the call, her momentary burst of bravado quickly deflating. She really hoped Brett didn't mind.

Nicole didn't exactly have a ton of friends to rely on.

Brett wasn't thirsty, but he didn't want to disappoint his young host. "I'll have some of that bottled water." He had picked up Ethan from school and delivered him safely home after getting a frantic phone call from Nicole. Gigi had let them in, then retreated to the TV room to watch her afternoon stories. Now Ethan was entertaining Brett in his great-grandmother's cozy kitchen.

Ethan grabbed a bottle of water from the refrigerator door. Trying to open it, he twisted up his face in a gesture that stabbed Brett in the heart. His little brother Max used to make a face like that when he was struggling with something.

A mix of nostalgia for the brother he had lost and anger for the secret Nicole had kept, hollowed out his gut. No more waiting. First chance he got, Brett would convince Nicole to allow Ethan to know Brett was his uncle. He just hoped she'd go along willingly.

Ethan twisted the cap off and handed the water to Brett. "Would you like anything to eat? Gigi made some cookies for me. There's a few left." He shuffle-slid in his socks across the worn linoleum floor and returned with a plate of cookies.

Brett took a cookie and bit into it. "Mmm. These are really good."

Ethan poured himself a glass of milk and slipped into the chair across from Brett at the kitchen table. Ethan took a cookie and proceeded to dip it into his milk. He caught Brett watching him. "Are you sure you don't want milk?"

Brett smiled and lifted his bottle of water. "I'm good. You're pretty independent for a little kid."

"I'm not that little." Indignation edged his voice. "Why couldn't my mom get me from school?" Ethan asked the question that had obviously been on his young mind since Brett's police cruiser pulled up outside the school and his teacher rushed him outside. "Is my mom in some kind of trouble?"

Brett studied the little boy. "No. She got stuck at work, and when your school called she didn't have a car to get you."

"Oh." Ethan seemed to consider his reply.

Brett leaned in close. "Why would you think your mother was in trouble?"

Ethan glanced toward the TV room. "A kid in my class said my mother was a troublemaker and his mom wouldn't let him come over to my house to play." Ethan shrugged. "I told him he was a liar." Ethan dipped a second cookie into the milk and his lips tugged down at the corners. A kid didn't forget when another kid bad-mouthed his mother.

"Is that why you missed the bus?"

Ethan's eyes widened, as if he was surprised Brett had figured him out. "I didn't mean to miss the bus…well, I just didn't feel like listening to this kid. He bugs me on the bus."

"With friends like that, who needs enemies?"

Ethan squinted at him, confused.

"A kid who says stuff like that, isn't your friend. Just ignore him."

"Yeah, that's what Gigi said." Ethan lowered his voice. "She also told me not to tell my mom because it would hurt her feelings."

Something twisted in Brett's heart. Ethan seemed years beyond his age.

"Your mom's feelings might be hurt, but I'm also pretty sure your mom would want you to tell her if something bothered you."

Ethan snapped a corner off his cookie. A smattering of crumbs sprinkled onto the table. "No, it doesn't bother me. Not anymore. I put a snowball in Joey's boot in his locker. I bet his foot got wet when he put it on."

Brett stifled a grin. As the chief of police, the last thing he wanted to do was encourage bad behavior. But he had to admit, the kid had spunk. He was tough. Sometimes tough was good, especially when a kid was defending his mom.

The sound of the front door opening signaled Nicole's return. She strolled into the kitchen and kissed Ethan's head.

She lifted her brown eyes to meet Brett's. "Thank you so much. I'm sorry if I interrupted your day. You didn't need to stay. Gigi's home." A flash of alarm lit her eyes. "Gigi's home, right?"

"She's watching her stories," Ethan said around another bite of cookie, sounding like a mature soul in a little kid's body. "Chief Eggert and I are having milk and cookies."

Nicole's eyes narrowed and she tucked a strand of hair behind her ear. "So, what have you two been talking about?"

"Guy stuff," Brett said. He pushed away from the table and stood. "But I should be going."

Nicole nodded. "Thanks again."

"Stay out of trouble, little man," Brett said.

Ethan's eyes opened wide and he nodded.

Brett tipped his head toward the front door, hoping she'd follow him. When she did, he leaned in close. "We need to talk."

"What?" The smooth skin on her forehead creased.

"Not here. Somewhere private." This conversation was long overdue.

* * *

Nicole made sure Ethan and Gigi had dinner before she headed out. She and Brett had far more to discuss than what they could cover in dribs and drabs while in her grandmother's kitchen. Worried little ears would be listening in.

Brett had said he'd pick her up after his shift ended around seven. Something in his tone when he left her house earlier had set her on edge.

What did Brett need to talk to her about?

Before then, Nicole had some business to take care of. She walked the few blocks to the funeral home, constantly aware of her surroundings. She was grateful for the few stragglers on Main Street, however if the ice incident had taught her anything, whoever had it out for her didn't care what time of day it was.

When she reached the funeral home, she felt like a kid sneaking onto the school grounds after hours. If anyone tried to stop her, she'd show them the clothes she was dropping off for Missy.

Nicole headed downstairs. She sucked in a quick breath when she realized Gene was down there. She had hoped to get in and out of the funeral home without running into anyone. She averted her eyes, not yet willing to learn if the body he was preparing was Missy's. She placed the bag with the sweater and Missy's favorite long skirt on the table.

Tears burned the back of her throat and she let out a long breath, trying not to breathe in the sweet scent unique to the cool basement of a funeral home. "Missy's clothes are here."

Gene nodded. "I heard you're going on vacation," he said in a low monotone voice, never lifting his head from his work.

She tried not to bristle. "Yeah, something like that."

"You'll be missed." He put a tool down on the metal table with a clack.

"Thank you. I'm going to grab my makeup and supplies from the cabinet." She couldn't afford to replace the expensive kit if it went missing. Her stomach tightened. Or if she lost this job for good. "Did Derreck say anything about me doing Missy's hair and makeup?"

Gene shrugged and kept working.

Nicole grabbed the makeup kit by its handle and set it down on the metal table. She opened the lid and pulled out the top two trays. Something shiny caught her eye. Her pulse thumped in her hears and she blinked rapidly against the walls that seemed to breathe on their own.

She reached in and pulled out a ruby ring. It had belonged to Mrs. Fenster—the woman she had worked on the other day.

Nicole peered over her shoulder. Gene was studying her. *Now, he decides to stop working and pay attention to me.* The adrenaline surging through her veins made her knees weak. She cleared her throat and suddenly realized Gene had been talking to her.

"What was that?" she asked, hoping he couldn't detect the tremble in her voice. She dropped the ring back into her makeup case.

"Are you going someplace warm?"

She snapped the trays back into place, concealing the ring. "Someplace warm?" She turned around to face him.

"For vacation?"

She shook her head, trying to clear it. "No, Ethan has school. I'll just catch up on things at home."

Nicole clicked the lid of the makeup kit closed and slid it off the table. "I better go." She swallowed around a lump in her throat and strode to the basement door.

"Nicole?"

"Yes?" She slowed her pace. Her mouth went dry.

"Is something wrong?" Gene's tone held a sympathy she didn't know was possible. He was usually cold, indifferent.

Nicole met his gaze and wished she could read the thoughts behind his cool gray eyes. "I'm just tired, Gene. And sad."

"About Missy."

"Yes, about Missy." Nicole hadn't really considered how Missy's death had affected Gene or anyone else at the funeral home.

"I liked Missy."

"Me, too." A tear slipped down her cheek. Nicole pushed through the basement door and climbed the steps. Grief and fear clouded her vision.

The thought of Mrs. Fenster's ring in her makeup kit burned fear into her heart. Someone was setting her up. Making her look guilty. Dishonest. A liar.

All the things she had been called as a teenager.

Who would want to do that to her?

The drug dealer she testified against. It had to be. She'd have to have Brett confirm he was still in prison. But how would he have access to her things?

Nicole glanced down at the basement door. What if he had friends?

A cold knot of fear formed in her gut. She couldn't risk going to jail and losing her son. She had to get Ethan. Leave Silver Lake.

No, no, no. She couldn't run. She had to learn to trust. She had to turn to the only person who could help her.

Or ruin her.

Brett decided to run home and change before picking up Nicole. He didn't want to have this discussion while he was wearing his police uniform. He didn't want her to feel threatened or intimidated in any way. He wanted to talk to her as a friend.

He stepped into his small ranch home and slowed his pace, his senses on high alert. A subtle noise from the kitchen told him he wasn't alone. With his hand hovering over his gun he moved toward the sound. The high-pitched squeal of the kettle sounded on the stove. He angled his head to see into the kitchen.

His mother was opening and closing cabinets.

"Mother?"

She dropped her hands to her side. "Finally. Where do you keep the tea?"

Brett pointed to the cabinet over the stove. "I'll get it for you." He handed her a tea bag and watched her fix herself a cup of tea. "What are you doing here?"

"I needed to talk to you and you've been avoiding my calls."

"I haven't been avoiding your calls. I've been working."

His mother pursed her lips. "What if your father or I had an emergency? Shouldn't the mother of the chief of police be able to get hold of her son?"

"If it's a true emergency—" he stressed *if* and *true* "—call 9-1-1." Brett slipped off his utility belt and put it down on the counter. He had been over this with his mother before. "Help would be there in minutes."

She made a harrumphing noise.

"Did you let yourself into my house because you had an emergency?"

"Yes." She tilted her chin ever so slightly.

Brett was skeptical. "Is everything okay?"

"No." She carried her cup and saucer over to the table and sat. Brett glanced at the clock on the wall, fully convinced he'd be late picking up Nicole. He was determined to clear the air with her tonight. If he was going to protect her, prove her innocence, there was no room for secrets between them.

"What's wrong?" He leaned his hip against the counter,

fearing that if he sat, his mother would take that as an invitation to extend her stay.

"You're spending time with *that* girl."

"What girl, Mother?" He knew exactly who his mother was referring to.

She shook her head and didn't give him an answer. As if saying her name would burn her lips. "She was no good for your brother. Look what happened to him. Don't fall into the same trap."

"I'm a big boy." He ran a hand across his whiskered jaw. He wondered if he'd have enough time to shave before he picked up Nicole.

"She's obviously promiscuous. She has a child and as far as I know she's never been married." Brett searched his mother's face, wondering if she had figured out Ethan was her grandson. Of course she hadn't, she was too busy hating Nicole.

"What would people say if the chief of police was dating a woman like her?" she continued.

"Mom, you were the one who taught me not to be judgmental."

His mother's lips twitched as if she was holding back a riot of words. "People talk."

The beauty of living in a small town.

"I've heard rumors." His mother lifted the teacup to her lips and took a long sip.

"I don't want to hear."

His mother set the cup in its saucer. "*That girl* has been stealing from the funeral home."

Brett bristled at the way his mother referred to Nicole.

"Rumors, that's all they are." He fisted his hands, then forced himself to relax them. "Is that what you came here to tell me? About a rumor?"

"Is it true? Are you investigating her?"

Brett sat next to his mother. He covered her hand and squeezed it. "I can't talk about work with you."

Not one to be told no, his mother pulled back her hand. "That girl got away with murdering my son. *Your brother.* She's walking around town like she owns the place. This is your chance to put her in jail." She leaned in close. He could smell her familiar perfume, the one that had made him feel alternately secure and powerless while he was growing up. His mother was one to handle things. Fix things.

Control things.

"If she's guilty of a crime, I'll seek justice." Deep down, he couldn't imagine Nicole guilty of anything but trying to get by in life. Or maybe he didn't want to imagine her capable of anything evil.

Did Nicole deserve his trust? He had learned trusting someone who didn't deserve it came at a price. His brother taught him that lesson.

"Promise me you won't let personal feelings get in the way of investigating *her.*"

He narrowed his gaze. "I always do my job." It was the one thing that gave him a sense of control.

His mother stood. A fire sparked in her eyes. "Make sure you do." She bowed her head. "Your brother's death changed me. I thought I was a forgiving person. But I can't seem to forgive that woman."

"Max's death changed me, too." Brett had not set foot in a church since his brother's funeral. He alternated between blaming God and blaming himself.

SIX

The doorbell rang and tingles raced across Nicole's arms. Brett was here. She tossed aside the pencil and it landed on the newspaper opened to the Jumble puzzle. She hadn't been able to unscramble any of the words. She was too distracted. Drawing in a deep breath, she stood and straightened the dish towel draped over the handle of the oven and ran a hand down the thigh of her jeans.

When she had arrived home from the funeral home, she'd changed clothes—three times. She knew full well this wasn't a date, but she felt compelled to look good for Brett. Silly, really. She hadn't had the opportunity to dress up for someone in a long time.

Too bad the man waiting at the door might think she was a thief. The ring she found in her makeup kit wouldn't do anything to dispel that. Maybe she shouldn't tell Brett about the ring. Unease twisted her stomach. Whoever hid the ring in her makeup kit was waiting to trap her in a lie.

The doorbell chimed again. A mix of dread and anticipation raced from her fingertips straight to her heart. She patted the tiny lump in her pocket. Mrs. Fenster's ring.

What if Brett didn't believe her?

What if he *did* believe her, arrested the guilty party, and she and Brett moved on to another level in their relationship?

Was it worth the risk of trusting him?

She couldn't think straight. Was this why he wanted to talk to her? Maybe his visit had nothing to do with the jewelry at all. Maybe he had more questions about Ethan.

She hustled down the hallway to the front door and sent up a quick prayer. *Please help me make the right decision...about everything. Please let Brett see the truth.*

Her grandmother knew Nicole was headed out for the evening. To make things easier, Nicole had already tucked in Ethan for the night. The last time she passed his bedroom, a light glowed from under his covers, evidence he was engrossed in a comic book.

She opened the front door and smiled. She couldn't help herself. Brett wore jeans and a ski jacket. He seemed relaxed. Healthy. Handsome.

A few bricks toppled off the wall she had carefully layered around her heart.

A smile pulled at the corners of his mouth, slightly tentative, as if he were as nervous as she. A few more bricks crumbled.

"Hey there," he said, his voice smooth and inviting.

"Hi."

Brett tipped his head. "Are you going to invite me in?"

Heat warmed her cheeks. She stepped back. "Of course. Come in a second while I grab my coat."

She opened the front door wider. From the back of the house she heard a thud, then little feet on the hardwood floor. Ethan peeked around the corner, hiding behind the kitchen wall.

"Come on. If you're not in bed you might as well say hello to Chief Eggert."

Ethan ran toward her with his open comic book flapping from his hand. "How come you don't have on your police uniform?" Ethan cut right to the chase. Kids were honest like that.

Brett's eyes softened. "Because I'm not working."

Ethan's little forehead crinkled. "Then why are you here?"

"Ethan…" Nicole scolded, keenly aware of Brett's gaze on her. "Don't be rude."

"Your mother and I are going to go out—"

"On a date!"

"Ethan!" Nicole was not going to win on this one.

"Are you going bowling?"

Brett laughed, a genuine sound that warmed Nicole's heart. "Bowling. I haven't gone bowling in years. No, I'm afraid we're not going bowling."

"I want to go bowling. My friend James had a bowling party but I couldn't go because Mom had to work and Gigi couldn't drive me there." Ethan's face scrunched up as if the pain was fresh.

"Ethan, I told you we'd try to go bowling another time." Nicole stuffed her arms into her coat. "He's never going to let me forget about that." The guilt of a single parent seemed never-ending. "Did you know I used to bowl in high school?" she asked mostly to Ethan, to lighten the mood.

"Yes." Ethan smiled, revealing his wiggly top tooth. "And you were really good."

"I never said I was really good." She zipped up her coat. "Did I?"

Brett placed a hand on the small of her back. "You're a bowler, huh? Good to know." He lifted an eyebrow, and unless she was mistaken, she detected a twinkle in his eye. Man, this was going to make what she had to tell him even harder. Would he still look at her like that, or would the fun, flirtatious look be replaced by one filled with disappointment and doubt?

Nicole smiled, her heart slowly sinking. She leaned over and kissed her son on the top of his head. She'd never tire of the smell of the no-tears shampoo. "Climb back into bed. Gigi's in the family room. Don't pester her. You're supposed to be asleep already." She pointed at him playfully. "I'll be back soon. You know my cell phone number for *emergencies*."

"Okay. 'Night, Chief Eggert." Ethan spun on the balls of his feet, sending his comic book flapping behind him as he raced to his bedroom. She strained an ear to listen for the thud and the creak that indicated he had dived into his bed.

Once Nicole and Brett got outside he said, "I'd like to talk to you in private. Without interruptions. Perhaps you wouldn't mind taking a drive with me."

Nicole felt the ring in her pocket. Her pulse beat frantically in her head, as if her world was about to implode.

What was so urgent that he had to talk to her in private? *Did* he know about the ring she found in her makeup case or was it something else?

She drew in a deep breath. No matter what Brett already knew, it was confession time for her.

"Privacy would be good. There's something I need to share with you, too."

Brett found himself driving through Silver Lake. Roads he had driven a million times before. He knew them better than he knew what was in his own heart most of the time.

He found himself heading toward the high school. Nicole was silent and he wondered if she was working up the nerve to tell him about Ethan. Was that what she had intended to share with him? He hoped so, because then he wouldn't be forced to bring up the subject.

He turned his pickup truck onto the long driveway leading to the school. He hadn't planned it, but suddenly it seemed like a good idea. Returning to the past so they could move forward.

Brett found a parking space next to the football field and turned off the ignition. They sat in silence as the temperature in the cab dropped quickly and the windows fogged up.

The light from the lamppost cast a gleam in Nicole's eyes. "Chief Eggert, if I didn't know you better, I'd think you were taking me parking."

"Parking?" He laughed, easing some of the tension that hung heavy between them. "I don't think I took a girl parking when I was a teenager. I was always the good boy. The choir boy."

"Not like your brother." Nicole's voice sounded very small, despite the fact that she was sitting only a few feet from him. Nicole laughed as if at a private joke she didn't find funny anymore. "I need to talk to you about something and I'm afraid." Her voice trembled over the last few words.

"I know."

Nicole jerked her head back. "What? You know?" She twisted her hands in her lap. "How…?"

"The resemblance."

Nicole shifted in her seat to face him, tilting her head, a look of understanding and maybe relief dawning in her eyes. "I'm surprised you didn't say something sooner."

"So, Ethan *is* my brother's son?"

"Can we take a walk?" Without waiting for an answer, Nicole slipped out of the truck. Brett got out and followed her across the snow to the bleachers. She brushed off a section of the metal bench and plopped down. Leaning forward, she rested her elbows on her thighs and stared off into the distance.

Brett sat next to her and followed her gaze. A few lonely lights lit the snow-covered football field. He turned to face her. "Ethan's my nephew, isn't he?" Brett wanted to pull Nicole into an embrace, while at the same time he wanted to shake the answer out of her.

Nicole slowly turned to meet his gaze, her eyes glistening in the moonlight. "Yes, Ethan is your nephew."

Hurt and something else—something he couldn't define—pierced his heart. "Why did you keep it a secret?" After Max's death, his family had not made it easy for Nicole to approach them. He closed his eyes briefly, sorry for the time lost with his nephew. His brother's son.

She crossed her arms and tucked her hands under her armpits. "I have to tell you about the night your brother died."

Brett's heart skittered and he swallowed around a lump. "No. I already know." He didn't want to think about the night his brother died. About the night his brother got so high he wrapped his car around a tree. The night police officers knocked on his front door and told his parents their youngest son was dead. The night he realized his life would never be the same.

Brett released a quick breath. "That's in the past." His words rang hollow in his ears. Not everyone had moved on since his brother's tragic death. Yet, he wanted to…he needed to. And he didn't need Nicole's apology. The cold from the metal bench bled through his jeans. He didn't want to relive that night. Not anymore.

"Nicole, I forgive you."

She winced. "I didn't ask for your forgiveness."

His chest tightened. "I don't want to talk about that night."

"I do. You don't know the truth. Not all of it. We have to clear the air, otherwise the past will always haunt me. Haunt us." She braced her arms on either side of her. Her pink mittens wrapped around the edge of the bleacher. Her voice grew softer. "I was not doing drugs the night your brother died. I hadn't done drugs in a long time."

Brett's pulse beat in his ears as he struggled to hear her soft words.

"Max had come over to my house to meet his dealer. Your parents were home and he said you were on his case.

Max said he couldn't sneeze without you offering him a tissue."

"I wasn't on his case *enough*." Guilt, his constant companion, needled him once again. "I believed my brother when he told me he had put drugs behind him. I wasn't watching him closely enough. I let my parents down. I let Max down."

Nicole stared straight ahead as if lost in thought. Her breath floated out in white clouds and hung suspended before dissipating in the frigid night air. A tear slid down her cheek. "Your brother was convincing. He charmed me more than once with his lies." She shifted to face him. "You can't blame yourself. Max made his own choices. It's taken me a long time to come to that conclusion. But it's true. Max made a horrible choice that night."

Brett covered her hand with his. "I miss him."

Nicole nodded. "Max was always the life of the party." She shrugged. "I don't think I really knew him." She pulled her hand out from under his. "I need to tell you something else."

"What?"

"When Max came to see me that night, I was so happy to see him." A faraway look descended into her eyes. "My happiness was short-lived. Max was high. He was slurring his words. Before I had a chance to talk some sense into him, sober him up, his dealer came over. We got into a huge argument. Oh, I was so mad, I told him I never wanted to see him again." She drew in a deep breath and let it out. "I thought maybe that would knock some sense into him."

Nicole tilted her face, as if trying to keep the tears from falling. Any words of comfort were lodged in his throat. All these years, and he had never heard Nicole's side of the story. His parents had solidly defined the narrative of that night. Nicole had supplied their son with drugs and let him drive away, high as a kite.

They sat in silence watching thick snowflakes fall from clouds that now masked the moon and stars. After Brett was able to swallow his emotions, he said, "I blame myself. I should have seen what was going on with my brother. Our whole family stuck our heads in the sand. We took the 'not my son, not my brother' attitude."

She shifted away from him, hiding her face. "That night..." She sniffed. "I was screaming at him as he got into the car. I knew he was in no condition to drive. When he rolled down the window, I grabbed on to the door frame. He didn't stop."

Brett put his hand on her knee. She flinched. "Don't blame yourself."

She turned to face him. "There I was, hanging on to the door frame and I screamed at him. I told him I was pregnant." She closed her eyes.

Brett's heart seized and he held his breath, waiting for Nicole to continue.

"That was the first time he learned I was pregnant and he didn't even stop. He didn't even look at me." She swallowed hard. "He gunned the car. I fell onto the driveway and smacked my head. My grandmother rushed me to the hospital."

Heat washed over him. The past reframed.

Brett couldn't breathe.

Nicole's throat ached. Her most carefully kept secret had been revealed, leaving her feeling exposed, scared, drained. She pulled up her collar and hunched her shoulders, trying to stay warm as the wind blew across the football field.

Brett sat next to her. He hadn't said a word since she'd told him about Max's last few moments on Earth. She dragged the toe of her boot back and forth in a line in the freshly fallen snow. After all the lies that had been told, would Brett believe her when she finally told him about the ring she had found in her makeup kit?

She stood and rested her elbows on the railing overlooking the football field. Nicole had never been in the bleachers, even in high school. She'd never hung with the rah-rah-school-spirit crowd. She always lived on the outside looking in.

Brett put his hand on the small of her back. "You were afraid to approach my family to tell them about the baby." Pain was evident in his voice.

"I was eighteen, pregnant, single, and the baby's father…"

"Had been killed in a car accident after partying with you." Brett finished her sentence.

"After everyone *assumed* he had been partying with me." She huffed and shook her head. "When I went into the hospital after falling from Max's car, I had a concussion. The doctor kept me overnight for observation, especially because of my pregnancy. When a story started to circulate that I had been admitted because of a drug overdose, I decided not to fight it. I convinced my grandmother not to say anything either."

"I don't understand. You allowed people to ruin your reputation."

Nicole pulled off her mitten and scratched her upper lip, then stuffed her hand back into her damp glove. What she wouldn't do for some hot chocolate and a thicker coat right now. "I had done plenty in my youth to ruin my own reputation. I decided that bad-mouthing Max was in no one's best interest. He wasn't here to defend himself. Besides, he paid the ultimate price."

She turned around and leaned against the railing. "This

was my chance to start over. To leave town and go someplace where no one would judge me based on my past."

"You deprived my parents of their grandson." Brett's deep voice rumbled through her.

Nicole shifted and stared at him, his face heavily shadowed. How could she make him understand? "I was afraid your family would take him from me. Ethan is all I have."

Brett dragged his finger along the edge of her coat sleeve. "Why?"

"My mother lost custody of me to my grandmother when I was ten. Why was it so unbelievable to think I feared the same thing? I was afraid no one would believe I had cleaned up my act." Tears burned the backs of her eyes. Her fear morphed to compassion. Her heart ached. "I'm sorry I didn't tell you your brother had a son. I was afraid."

"Hasn't Ethan asked about his father?"

"Sure. I told him his father died in a car accident before he was born. I left out the details, of course." Nicole was keenly aware of Brett studying her. "I told him his father was in heaven watching over him." She cleared the knot of grief in her throat. "He's only seven. It seemed enough information until he got older."

"This is incredible. Max had a son."

She sniffed and bounced on the balls of her not-thick-enough boots. "Please forgive me." She did want his forgiveness after all. "Ethan was all I had left and I couldn't lose him, too."

"I'm sorry my family made you feel like you had to keep Ethan a secret." Brett laughed, a nervous sound. "I know my parents can be pretty intimidating."

Nicole lifted her eyebrows. "You think?"

Brett tipped his head, then grabbed her hand and squeezed. "Can I get to know Ethan?"

Nicole bit her lower lip. "I've never told him much about

his father." Panic welled in her chest. "I'm afraid your family would tell Ethan the truth. About my misspent youth." She laughed, but it sounded pathetic. Panicky. "You don't think they'd try to take him away from me?" Voicing her concern out loud made it seem ludicrous. But she couldn't squash her fears.

"No. You are a good mother. Anyone can see that." They locked eyes and stayed quiet like that for a long moment. "Let my family get to know Ethan. *Please.*"

Nicole glanced down, a knot of emotion trapping her words.

"Trust me,"

Nicole was the first to break the connection. Could she trust him? Did she have a choice?

"You could have told my family the truth about the night Max died. Why didn't you?" Brett braced his hands against the railing.

"No one would have believed me." That was the truth. "And I thought it would hurt your family more than help." She drew in a deep breath. Off in the distance, a critter raced across the football field at the fifty-yard line. "I did blame myself in some ways. Either way, nothing I could say would have brought back Max. And I had planned to make a new life outside of Silver Lake. I thought it was the compassionate thing to do." And the safer thing if she wanted to keep Ethan to herself.

"And in case you forgot, your father is a formidable man. He would have made my life—and my grandmother's life—miserable had I stayed. It was easier all around if I left. It was the proverbial clean slate."

"My parents were really hurting." Nicole understood Brett needed to justify his parents' anger. She was angry, too.

"There's something else I need to tell you. Something I need your help with." She had revealed her biggest secret, what was one more? She turned her back to Brett, unable to bear the pain in his eyes.

"What is it?" his gravelly voice sounded low in the darkness.

Nicole drew in a deep breath. A fluttery anxiety hollowed out her stomach. She yanked off her mitten, dug into her pocket and fingered the ring.

Mrs. Fenster's ring.

Her hand felt leaden as she pulled it out and unrolled her fingers to reveal the gold ring with a sizeable ruby stone. "I found this in the bottom of my makeup kit today."

"A ring?"

"Yes, it belonged to Mrs. Fenster. We buried her recently." She pressed the ring into the palm of his leather glove. "Take it. Give it back to her family." She slipped on her mitten and squeezed the metal rail. "Someone is trying to make it look like I'm stealing from the funeral home."

Brett put the ring in his pocket and moved next to her, leaning a hip on the railing. "Why would someone frame you?" Was that skepticism she detected in his voice? Anger heated her cheeks. He still didn't trust her.

Nicole pressed her lips together and her eyes narrowed. "You don't believe me."

"I didn't say that." He lowered his voice and stepped closer. "I'm trying to understand why someone would do this to you."

She crossed her arms and ran her mittens up and down her arms. The cold had seeped into her bones and she feared she'd never, ever get warm again.

"The only person that would have it in for me is Richard White, the drug dealer I testified against." Numb lips made it difficult to form the words. "Did you make sure he's still in prison?"

"I checked. White was released four months ago."

"What?" Her pulse roared in her ears. "He shouldn't be out. Why didn't anyone tell me?"

"Early parole. Records show he's staying with his mother in Central New York. I have a call into his parole officer to double check on his status."

"Why didn't you tell me?" Nicole's tone was bordering on hysteria.

"I'm telling you now. And I wanted to have concrete information before I raised any red flags. You have enough stress in your life right now."

Nicole pressed her fingers to her temples, a killer headache pulsing behind her eyes.

"Nicole," Brett said, his tone hesitant, "how would White have access to your makeup kit?"

She shook her head, icy dread pooling in her stomach. "I don't know."

Brett wrapped his arm around Nicole and led her toward the truck, following the same path that had brought them to the bleachers. Brett opened the passenger side for her, then walked around, got in, turned the key in the ignition and cranked the heat. He shifted in his seat to face her.

"We'll get to the bottom of this."

Hope blossomed on her face. "You believe me?"

"My job is to find the truth."

Nicole sighed and slumped into the seat. "The truth is, I'm innocent." Whether he believed her or not, she wasn't going to run anymore. She had done that eight years ago and had regretted it ever since. "I'm going to stay and prove my innocence, no matter what the cost."

Gray clouds shrouded the cemetery. A small group, including Missy's mother and a minister, gathered under a green tent. The lavender casket was mounted on a steel structure above an opening in the earth that was to be Missy's final resting place.

Nicole's chest ached from the cold and her grief. She swallowed around the tears clogging her throat. She rested her hands on Ethan's shoulders. Her little man had insisted on saying his goodbyes to mommy's friend who had always taken the time to play Monopoly with him—and not the short version, either.

Brett stood next to her, dressed smartly in his police uniform. They hadn't talked much since the other night at the football field when she finally told him Ethan was his nephew. At some point, she'd have to tell Ethan. Brett and she had agreed to wait until after the funeral. She kissed her son's head and smoothed his hair. She prayed she'd done the right thing.

It didn't matter, she supposed. Her gaze drifted to Missy's casket. Someday they'd all be dead and in the ground. A whisper of dread washed over her and she suddenly felt very, very cold. Her skin prickled as if someone was watching her.

The minister raised his voice, indicating he was ready to start. He recited some nice words—generic words—meant for the deceased he had never met. Nicole was too grief stricken to be upset by this. The poor minister was probably called many times a week to recite prayers for people who'd never felt the need to go to church when life was good.

Nicole bowed her head and said a quiet prayer for her friend.

When she raised her head, the sense someone was watching intensified. She scanned the gray stones marking the burial spots for the hundreds—thousands—of former Silver Lake residents. She squeezed Ethan's shoulders tighter. He wiggled out from under her and moved next to Brett, apparently annoyed when her possessive grasp had dug into his shoulders through his winter jacket.

Brett placed his hand on his nephew's shoulder and he

didn't budge. An unexpected surge of jealousy further darkened her mood.

When the service ended, Nicole lingered by the casket. She placed a pink rose on top of the pile of pink roses. Nicole kissed her fingers, then pressed them to the cold, smooth surface of the casket. "Love you."

Nicole turned around and found Brett consoling Mrs. Flowers. Beyond them, the tent was empty. Her heart stuttered. Ethan was gone.

He couldn't have gone far.

She scanned farther out, beyond the tent area. No sign of him. There was probably a reasonable explanation. What seven-year-old boy wouldn't want to explore a big old cemetery? He was probably fine, but her momma-bear instincts made her hyperaware of her surroundings and eager to find her son.

Her unease intensified. Her boots crunched on the packed snow. She followed a set of footprints that branched off on their own. She swallowed around a lump in her throat.

If Brett didn't think she was an incompetent parent before, he'd surely think she was now. The gray clouds hunkered in closer. White flakes fell from the sky.

Ethan loved snow.

Another set of tracks joined the single set and wound through the cemetery around ornate statues of angels, crosses and doves. The rush of adrenaline made her stomach hurt.

At her wit's end, Nicole was about to call for her son when she spotted him. He stood twenty feet away talking to a man dressed in gray work pants and a thick winter jacket with orange reflective markings. The man had his back to her and he was leaning on a shovel.

The snowflakes swirled in a disorienting pattern in front of her eyes. She blinked them away.

Nicole broke into a jog. "Ethan, come on. It's time to go."

The man slowly turned around. "Hello, Nicole."

Her vision tunneled. Tiny stars exploded around the periphery. Standing in front of her was Richard White, Max's drug dealer. The man she had testified against.

So much for being with his mother in Central New York.

She reached out and grabbed Ethan's arm. "Come on. Chief Eggert is waiting for us."

"You know this man, Mommy?"

Words jammed in her throat.

"Yeah, Mommy, why don't you tell your dear son how you know me?" Richard slowly turned around and jabbed at the earth with his shovel.

"Come on, Ethan. We can't keep the *chief of police* waiting." She locked eyes with Richard, wanting him to fully register the reality that Brett was watching out for her. Protecting her.

She grabbed Ethan's hand and pulled him harder than she had intended. He stumbled over the corner of a tombstone. When she slowed to steady him, her eyes caught the name carved on the stone: *Maxwell Ethan Eggert. Son and brother taken too soon.*

Nicole froze. Ethan's father's grave. Her stomach plummeted. Each snowflake floated slowly down, landing on the wide gray granite. As if in slow motion, she turned to face Ethan.

His eyes rounded, sensing her fear. He was watching her, not the gravestone. "What's wrong, Mommy?"

She shook away her trance. "We have to go. Chief Eggert is waiting for us."

Nicole tugged her son's arm, desperation making her act unreasonably. "Mom, you're hurting my arm."

"Yeah, *Mom*," Richard said, his voice a creepy mix of humor and darkness. "You don't want to hurt the boy."

Not dignifying him with an answer, she leaned in close to Ethan. "I'm sorry. But we have to go."

When she reached Brett's cruiser, she pulled on the door handle. It was locked. Ethan slipped his hand out of hers. "Why did you do that? That man wanted to tell me something."

"How many times have I told you not to talk to strangers? You don't go running off with someone." She fisted her hands. Had all her stranger-danger speeches landed on deaf ears?

Ethan rolled his eyes in dramatic fashion. "I could see you and Chief Eggert the whole time. Who's going to hurt a little kid when the police are there?"

Nicole couldn't catch her breath. "Don't talk to that man ever again. He's bad."

"Why, Mom?" His forehead crinkled.

She straightened and watched Brett approaching with his cell phone pressed to his ear. Across the cemetery, Richard was sitting on Max's tombstone, watching her.

"He's a bad man. Trust me."

SEVEN

Brett draped his arm over the back of the hard plastic chair. The thunderous crash of bowling balls striking pins filled the bowling alley. The smell of greasy food, oily lanes and shoe disinfectant brought back memories of his teen years. There wasn't a lot to do in a small town. Bowling was something to do.

Nicole placed her hand on Ethan's shoulder and gave him pointers. Her son wiggled his shoulders and scooted forward, eager to throw the ball down the lane. His way. He pulled back his arm and flung the green-marbled ball. The ball bounced off the bumper guard on the right, hooked left, and bounced off the opposite side. When the ball limped toward the pins, it only had enough momentum to knock down two.

Ethan spun around and pumped his fist. He had a huge smile on his face. "Did you see that?"

Nicole held up her hand for a high five. "Awesome."

Ethan smacked his mom's hand then Brett's gaze connected with Nicole's. He had given her some distance in the days following Missy's funeral. In that time, he had done some digging and found out Richard White, the man Nicole had testified against, had left his mother's home and had been working for the cemetery for about three months.

Brett now had a prime suspect. Who better to harass Nicole than the man she had put behind bars? But to date, Brett had no proof. When he had driven out to the cemetery to talk to Richard, the man claimed he wanted nothing more than to get his life back on track. And as far as talking to the kid went, he'd thought Ethan would like to see where his dad was buried.

Brett still got angry when he envisioned Richard's cocky smirk. Brett knew Richard wanted to intimidate Nicole. Show her he was back. That he could reach her son, if he chose to.

But nothing would happen to Ethan or Nicole. Brett would make sure of it.

Ethan grabbed his ball the minute the ball return released it. He stuck his tongue out the corner of his mouth. Max used to do that.

Nostalgia and loss twisted Brett's insides. He wished he had spent more time with his little brother instead of pushing him away, as older brothers tended to do. Maybe things would have turned out differently.

Nicole brushed past Ethan and picked up her bowling ball. He was impressed that she actually owned one, as well as shoes. "It's my turn, little man."

Ethan frowned, then flopped down next to Brett. Brett nudged him on the shoulder. "Your mom is really good."

Ethan smiled, pushing his tongue against his loose tooth. "Anyone can knock down pins with those bumper guard things."

"Hey, thanks a lot. I heard that." Nicole stood waiting for her bowling ball, tapping her fingers on the top of the tunnel where it would pop out.

He and Nicole had decided they'd tell Ethan that Brett was his uncle tonight—if the night went well—otherwise they'd wait. He wondered if she was as nervous as he was.

Brett watched Nicole—her back to him as she approached the lane—wiggle her shoulders as she lined up the ball with the pins. He had been watching her all night. She had a graceful way about her. She drew her arm back and released the ball. It landed with a thud and moved

Plus 2 FREE Mystery Gifts!

2 FREE BOOKS

ABSOLUTELY FREE · GUARANTEED

CLAIM YOUR FREE GIFTS

YES! Please send me my **2 FREE BOOKS** and **2 FREE GIFTS.** I understand that, as explained on the back of this card, I am under no obligation to purchase anything!

Affix sticker here

2 FREE Books

M-8801-0792-MG

❏ I prefer the regular-print edition
153/353 IDL GGAA

❏ I prefer the larger-print edition
107/307 IDL GGAA

FIRST NAME

LAST NAME

ADDRESS

APT.#

CITY

STATE/PROV.

ZIP/POSTAL CODE

swiftly toward the pins. The pins exploded and Nicole spun around, mimicking her son's fist pump. "Boo-yah."

It warmed Brett's heart to see Nicole so happy, carefree. Brett patted Ethan's shoulder. "Take my turn."

Ethan sprang up. "Thanks."

Ethan hefted the bowling ball to his chest. He palmed it until he found the finger holes. He did that tongue-sticking-out thing again and jammed his fingers into the finger holes. He seemed to be mentally calculating something, then he approached the lane. He lowered his arm and flung the ball forward. It rolled down the lane before taking a sharp right, bouncing alternately off each gutter bumper.

Ethan spun around, a huge smile on his face. "I'm having so much fun. Can we come again sometime?"

Nicole stood and hooked her finger under his chin. "Enjoy the here and now. Don't worry about next time."

Ethan seemed to consider his mother's words. "I'm having so much fun I don't want it to end."

Nicole caught Brett's eye and they both laughed. "Ah, to be a kid." Brett leaned in and whispered, "I'm having a lot of fun, too."

"Me, too," Nicole mouthed.

"I would never have guessed you were a bowler."

A fire lit her eyes. "I'm full of surprises."

"I bet."

Something flittered in the depths of her eyes, something he couldn't quite name. Nicole stepped away from him and spun around.

Ethan stuffed his hands in his jeans pockets, apparently oblivious to the moment Brett had shared with Nicole. "Can I get some pizza?"

The concession stand was located about twenty feet behind them across a worn royal-blue carpet with red and black diamonds. Brett dug into his pocket for money, but Nicole flicked her fingers at him. She opened her purse and handed Ethan a few dollars. "One piece and a small pop, okay?"

"Okay." Ethan grabbed the money and ran to wait in line. Nicole didn't take her eyes off him.

"I would have been happy to get you both something to eat."

"This is not a date," she whispered so as not to be overheard.

"No?" He smiled, enjoying the pink blossoming on her cheeks. "I thought you were having a good time?"

She fought the smile, but the smile won. "I am. I like seeing Ethan having a good time."

"Okay, fair enough. Can we call the next time we go out a date?" Brett ran his knuckle across the back of Nicole's hand.

"Stop, Ethan is right there."

Brett shook his head. "He's too busy trying to decide what kind of soda to have. Besides, we're not doing anything."

"You're incorrigible."

"I'm the chief of police."

Nicole rolled her eyes.

"Hasn't Ethan ever been exposed to the men in your life?"

Nicole shifted to meet his gaze. "First, you are not a man in my life. Second, I don't date."

"Not ever?"

She turned her attention back to Ethan. "Being a single mom doesn't allow much room. And being a single mom with a bad reputation doesn't leave much desire. I'm really trying to stay the course."

"You know I'm here for you. I'm going to help you through this. Find out for certain who is harassing you and put a stop to it. We'll be keeping an eye on Richard White."

Nicole let out a long breath. "So does that mean you

believe I didn't steal the jewelry that showed up in my makeup case?"

Brett watched Ethan hand the cashier his wadded-up money. "I spoke to Derreck at the funeral home. He said it's not unusual for them to leave the back door unlocked. Anyone could have gained access to the basement and your makeup case."

Nicole's eyes brightened. She placed her hand on his biceps, got up on tiptoes and brushed a kiss across his cheek. "Thank you. That means more than you know."

She quickly separated from Brett, her cheeks firing a bright pink. "Why hasn't some sweet girl scooped you up?"

"Too busy with the job, I suppose." Brett tried to sound flippant, but after the horrible picture his parents had painted of Nicole and the horrible things she had supposedly done to Max, he had a hard time trusting women. Sure, he dated, but he never let it get too far. Strange, the first time he was thinking about serious involved Nicole.

He traced her warm jaw. "Maybe it's time I took time."

"Oh, I d-don't know…" Nicole stammered.

"Hey, Mom, look at me." Ethan balanced a tray with a slice of pizza and a drink. His eyes grew wide when the cup slid toward the edge of the tray.

Nicole jumped up and grabbed everything from him. Ethan ran ahead and plopped down next to Brett. It was clear Nicole already had a man in her life. He just happened to be three foot something with a wiggly toothed grin.

It was hard to compete.

Agreeing to go bowling with Brett had been a mistake. A big fat mistake. Nicole drew in a deep breath.

Brett was the complete opposite of his younger brother. Max had been blond and stocky, and a chatterbox. Brett was tall, dark and a man of few words. Max was flighty, unreliable and immature. With Brett, words like *solid*, *dependable* and *trustworthy* came to mind.

Definitely good traits.

Someone a girl could fall in love with.

Someone Nicole could fall in love with.

If she was looking to fall in love.

She wasn't. The only male she loved was Ethan. Who at the moment was wolfing down a piece of pizza and chatting animatedly with Brett about bowling and his new strategy for knocking over more pins.

"Excuse me a minute," Nicole said, pointing at Ethan. "Stay here with Brett. I'll be right back."

"We'll be fine." Brett patted Ethan's back as her son wiped pizza sauce from his fingers.

"Can I take your turn, Mom?" Ethan jumped up and pointed at the overhead score sheet.

"Go for it." Nicole stepped up onto the blue carpet and paused. Ethan was smiling at Brett as he picked up his bowling ball. He never stopped talking the whole time. Her son had needed a male role model.

Nicole's gut twisted. Had she hurt more than helped Ethan by not letting Max's family into his life? She had held Ethan so close because she had been afraid of losing him. She ran a hand across her chin and let out a frustrated huff. She had too much going on right now to think straight.

She strode down the carpeted aisle, the sound of strikes, near strikes and disappointed whoops filling her ears. She had come here often as a teenager with her youth group on Saturday mornings. Before she had become too cool for bowling and the church youth group.

Before she started hanging out with the wrong people.

She shook away her rambling thoughts and hustled her step. The ladies' room was tucked away in the far corner of the building. She pushed open the door of the bathroom. The white cracked counters and blue chipped sinks hadn't been updated since her high school days.

Nicole leaned in to the mirror and tried to wipe the dark shadows from under her eyes. No such luck. Those half-moons of gray were permanent, something that only a few good nights of sleep—or heavy concealer—could erase. She smoothed a hand over her hair and wondered what Brett could possibly see in her. She was too pale, too thin and had too much baggage.

Her son. That's what Brett wanted.

The hard edge of doubt sliced through the warm confidence she had experienced only a few minutes ago. Her lack of self-confidence had always been her undoing.

Nicole rolled her shoulders and sighed. And she remembered her advice to her son. *Enjoy the here and now.* She'd have to learn to trust Brett. Trust that letting the Eggert family in wouldn't mean losing her son.

Nicole pushed open the stall door just as the lights went out, casting the windowless room into complete darkness. Her adrenaline spiked. Her pulse raced in her ears and drowned out any other sound. She clung to the lock on the stall door. Indecision had her rooted in place.

You're being silly. Maybe the power went out. That's all.

Distinct footsteps echoed off the cement walls.

Biting her lip to hold back the yelp clawing at her throat, Nicole stepped back into the stall and closed the door silently. She slid the lock into place knowing full well it wouldn't hold if someone *really* wanted to get to her.

Her mind went immediately to Ethan. He was safe, he had to be. He was with Brett. Brett would never let anything happen to him.

But what if the power had gone out in the entire bowling alley? What if someone took that opportunity to snatch Ethan?

Stop! She had to get hold of herself.

Nicole got on her tiptoes and hollered, "Who's there?" She tried to sound calm when she knew she sounded breathy, panicked. Out of her mind.

The footsteps grew closer.

Thump.

Thump.

Thump.

Silence. She sensed someone standing on the other side of the metal door. Goose bumps raced up her arms and made the fine hairs on the back of her neck stand up.

Dear Lord, protect me.

Nicole held on to the metal lock. The door shook violently. She swallowed her panic. Her sweaty grip slipped off the metal lock.

"Who's there?" Nicole repeated, her voice thin and squeaky. Weak.

A loud bang vibrated the door. Nicole jumped and the backs of her legs made contact with the cold, moist porcelain toilet bowl. *Yuck.* She pressed her palms against the cool metal side walls and kept herself from falling into the toilet water.

The footsteps retreated.

Her breathing sounded in her ears. Nicole waited for what seemed an eternity. She said a silent prayer of protection. She slid the lock. She pushed open the door, fully expecting to be attacked.

Nothing.

In the inky blackness, she dragged her hand along the outside of the stall doors. Across to the sink. Down the short hallway to the bathroom exit. Before her palm hit the door, she felt the light switch. She flicked it on then blinked against the glaring brightness.

So much for a power outage.

Her head told her to run. Tell Brett.

But curiosity got the best of her. She returned to the stall and saw a note taped to the door. Goose bumps raced across her skin.

I know where you work.
I know where you live.
I know where you play.

Brett stood in the doorway of Ethan's bedroom as Nicole brushed a kiss across her son's forehead and wished him good-night.

"'Night, Chief Brett," Ethan called out dreamily, sleep starting to sneak in. "I had a lot of fun tonight."

"Me, too, buddy. We'll do it again sometime."

"Promise?"

Brett didn't want to make a promise he couldn't keep. He searched Nicole's expression and she gave him a subtle nod.

"Of course. We'll do it again." Brett wanted to be a positive influence in this kid's life. He was a great kid, he just needed some guidance to avoid making some bad decisions in school. Right now, it was horseplay at the lunch table. In a few years, who knew what kind of trouble he could get into if he didn't have the right influence.

Nicole brushed past Brett. He could smell her shampoo; it smelled like cucumbers. He stepped into the hallway and she closed Ethan's bedroom door. She lifted her index finger to her pink lips and gestured for him to follow her down the hall.

When they reached the kitchen, he could hear the loud voices and laugh track from a sitcom floating in from the other room. "Gigi loves her programs." Nicole lowered her voice. "They're good company, I suppose. I guess now I'll be able to spend more time with her since Mr. Peters wants me to take a little vacation." She shook her head. The stress of the past few days was written on her face.

The kettle whistled. Nicole made them both tea and they sat across from each other at the small round table.

Nicole slumped as if she had the weight of the world on her shoulders. "I'm glad I was able to get Ethan home and to bed without him realizing what happened at the bowling alley," Nicole whispered. "And please, don't say anything to Gigi."

Brett nodded. "I'm sorry we didn't catch the guy." He had called Ed Hanson and the two of them searched all the back corners of the bowling alley. Really, it could have been anyone. Perhaps the person returned to bowling, seemingly innocent. They were specifically searching for Richard White, and he hadn't been seen anywhere around the bowling alley.

In a small town, a lot of people knew Richard and no one had seen him. When Ed checked White's house, he was home playing video games. But had he rushed home, making it back before the police arrived?

"You sure you didn't see anything? The person's shoes under the door. Anything?"

Nicole rested her forehead on the heel of her hand. "No. He turned the lights off." Her face looked pale. "What would have happened if I wasn't able to lock myself in the stall?"

The need to protect Nicole welled up inside him. "You can't—"

"What?" She straightened her back. "I can't leave my house until you figure out who's harassing me?" Anger flashed in her eyes. "That's not reasonable is it? I have a son who needs to go to school. A grandmother who needs groceries…" Her voice trailed off. "I suppose Mr. Peters did me a favor by making it unnecessary for me to go to work."

"I'm really worried this guy's contact with you is going to escalate."

Nicole bit her lower lip. "If it's Richard White and he wants to get even with me for putting him in jail, why not attack me? Hurt me. Get it over with." She jutted her chin out in a show of defiance, a flash of the teenager she used to be. "Why let a measly lock on a bathroom door stop him? Did he run my car off the road? Did he try to drop the icicles on me? It's like he's taking a step back. He's shifted from trying to seriously hurt me to taunting me. I don't get it."

Brett had wondered the same thing.

Nicole pushed away from the table and stood. "I don't think he wants to hurt me. I think whoever is doing this wants to scare me. Scare me away from Silver Lake, by making my life miserable."

Brett stared at her, apprehension pooling in the pit of his stomach. "I don't like that look in your eyes."

Nicole jerked her head back. "I can't let someone roll over me. Not like before."

"What do you mean?"

"I never stood up for myself. I was a young, stupid kid, and after your brother died, I thought the only solution was to leave town. Run away from all the accusations. Not defend myself."

Nicole pulled out the chair and sat. She reached across and pulled his hand between her chilly fingers. "I never told the truth because I figured it didn't matter. But the truth does matter. I'm not going to back down. I'm going to stand my ground."

Brett watched her intently, his heart rate kicking up a notch. "I'm sorry you had to go through that all alone."

She studied his face warily. "Thank you. And now you can understand why I'm not going to run away now. I have to stay. Protect my name."

"I'll help you."

A small smile tugged on her pink lips. "And I'm sorry

we weren't able to talk to Ethan tonight. To tell him you're his uncle."

"I'm sorry, too." Brett lifted his hand and brushed his thumb across her cheek. "I'm not going anywhere. We'll tell him soon. Together."

EIGHT

"I don't think this is a good idea." Nicole and Brett stood on Mr. and Mrs. Peters's front porch. She shifted from one foot to the other, partly to thaw out her toes, partly wanting to make a fast exit. "Last time I came here, I was forced to take a *vacation*." She rolled her eyes.

"We need to address the jewelry incident head-on or they might think you're hiding something."

Nicole had a distinct case of déjà vu, but hoped Brett's presence made a difference this time.

Nicole lifted her hand to knock on the Peterses' front door when it flew open. She stepped back, startled, and Brett placed his hands on her waist to steady her. Gene, the mortician, muttered a curt greeting and rushed past them and down the driveway. The door stood ajar, but neither Nicole nor Brett felt it was their rightful place to walk in.

Gene strode down the street. "I wonder what he was doing here. I thought he worked at the funeral home."

Nicole tapped her thigh, the urge to turn and run nearly overwhelming her. She drew in a deep breath. "That isn't exactly a full-time job. The Peterses always have him running errands and such. Similar to how I do hair and makeup *and* paperwork around the office." She watched Gene get into a beat-up old car under the shadow of a huge pine tree.

The home nurse, dressed in a crisp gray uniform, appeared in the open doorway. She had a curious expression on her face. "I didn't hear you ring."

"Gene was just leaving," Nicole said.

"Well, Mrs. Peters is resting in the sunroom. Please, come in." The middle-aged woman ushered them toward the back of the house, her cushy white shoes silent on the tile.

Mrs. Peters was sitting in the same chaise as the other day with a blanket draped over her legs. The elderly woman covered her mouth and coughed. Her eyes, with just a shadow of their usual feistiness, registered their presence. "To what do I owe this visit? The chief of police himself." Mrs. Peters's gaze drifted past Nicole without acknowledging her.

Nicole felt a little light-headed. Had Mrs. Peters already made up her mind about her?

"How are you, Mrs. Peters?" Brett took off his hat and tucked it under his arm.

The blanket twitched over Mrs. Peters's feet as if she was wiggling her toes. "I don't know what's worse, to lose one's body or one's mind." She lifted a shaky hand. "I'm sharp as a tack, but my body has failed me. But if I had lost my mind…" a wet, popping laugh bubbled up "…I wouldn't be any the wiser."

The nurse hovered in the doorway for a moment, then, as if on some unknown command, disappeared into one of the other rooms.

"Is Mr. Peters home?" Nicole clasped her hands in front of her and shifted her feet. Heat pooled under her arms. She fumbled with the buttons of her coat.

"He had to run out for a bit. I was in the mood for some ice cream." She gave Nicole a tight smile. "Is there something I can help you both with?"

"It has to do with the funeral home. How long before he gets back?" Brett asked. "It's important that we speak to him."

Mrs. Peters narrowed her gaze. "The funeral home is

my family business. My grandfather built it up from nothing."

"Quite an accomplishment." Brett cleared his throat. "It was my understanding that your husband was running the business now."

Nicole wondered if Brett was aware of the thin ice he was skating on. Mrs. Peters was obviously proud of her position within the company, and despite her poor health, she still relished her authority. That was obvious from Nicole's last visit.

Mrs. Peters waved her hand in a regal gesture, one that would have been even grander if her frail arm hadn't trembled. "Since my illness, my husband and now my nephew have taken over day-to-day operations. But if you need to discuss the family business, I am more than capable."

Brett cut Nicole a sideways glance. Nicole had a solid working relationship with Mr. Peters. At this point, she hated to bring up her concerns with Mrs. Peters, the more mercurial of the two.

Mrs. Peters swirled her hand in a get-on-with-it gesture.

"Before we get down to business, can you tell me why your employee Gene Gentry was here?" Brett asked.

Mrs. Peters jerked her head back as if offended by the question. Her gaze dropped to the vials lined up on the table next to her. "If you must know, he was bringing me my prescriptions. Why is this important to you?" She angled her chin and narrowed her eyes at him.

"My job is to ask questions."

"Did I do something wrong?" Mrs. Peters folded her hands in her lap and waited for the answer.

"Not at all."

Nicole threw a hard glare at Brett. What she had to say was hard enough without him riling up the frail woman. Nicole's palms grew slick. "I came here to tell you I am a trustworthy person."

Mrs. Peters narrowed her gaze. "There is usually a reason someone must defend their virtue. Did something else happen? Besides what I already know?"

"I found a ring in my makeup kit." Nicole felt as if her heart was going to explode in her chest.

"You found a ring...?" Mrs. Peters wrinkled her face. "I don't suppose it jumped in there."

Brett sat across from Mrs. Peters and leaned forward, resting his elbows on his thighs. "I believe someone is trying to cause problems for Nicole."

Mrs. Peters tugged on the throw covering her lap. "I have found, over my long life, that things are often as they appear. It's never very complicated."

Nicole slipped off her coat and draped it over her arm. Sweat dripped down her back. "I have never stolen anything—"

"Ever?" Mrs. Peters startled Nicole. She wasn't expecting such a sharp response from the frail woman.

Nicole hiked her chin and swallowed around a lump in her throat. "When I was a teenager I stole to feed my drug habit. I'm not the same person." Her skin prickled under Brett's intense gaze.

"Ah..." A smug expression settled on Mrs. Peters's wrinkled features. "People rarely change."

Nicole crossed her arms. "I have changed. I'm an honest, hardworking person. I would never steal from anyone. I need this job. You have to believe me."

Mrs. Peters's pale complexion turned a bright shade of red, as if a bucket of red paint had been poured over her head. "I don't have to do anything. That's the beauty of being old and sick. I'm afforded a certain amount of latitude."

Brett covered the woman's frail hand with his. The act of compassion seemed to come naturally to him. "I've gotten to know Nicole and her son since they've been back in Silver Lake. I believe her. But as chief of police, I will be investigating this fully."

Nicole's heart plummeted at Brett's subtle about-face. Did he believe she was innocent or not?

Mrs. Peters shook her head and tears filled her eyes as a violent cough racked her thin frame. Nicole turned to get the nurse and nearly ran into her. The woman must have been hovering nearby, ready to respond if necessary. She efficiently crossed the room and lifted a glass of water with a straw to the elderly woman's lips.

"I'm afraid Mrs. Peters must rest," the nurse said.

"We understand." Brett stood. "Can I ask you about your nephew, Derreck? How well do you know him?"

"Derreck is like a son to me." Mrs. Peters sat up a bit straighter. "I hope you're not harassing him."

"No, I'm just doing my job. I'm investigating a person from Nicole's past. A person who may wish to complicate her life. To cause problems for her."

"Who might that be?" Mrs. Peters struggled to clear her throat.

Brett's expression told Nicole he was debating whether or not he should say anything more. He turned back to Mrs. Peters. "Richard White recently got out of jail. It was Nicole who testified against him and put him there. I'm still gathering evidence, but he has reason to get back at Nicole."

Mrs. Peters ran shaky fingers across her thin lips. "The world is a crazy place."

"I'm asking that you have an open mind." Brett touched Mrs. Peters's shoulder. She angled her face toward him and smiled.

"You're a charmer, just like your father." Mrs. Peters patted his hand. "We went to high school together. Did you know that?"

Brett smiled. "Yes. I guess it's true what they say about a small town, everyone knows everyone."

Mrs. Peters's gaze drifted to Nicole. "Brett's father wasn't a fool. I'm afraid his sons may be drawn in by a pretty face. I'm not. I'd be a fool to trust this woman." Her gaze slowly slid to Brett. "Her dishonesty could ruin the funeral home my granddaddy founded."

Nicole pressed a hand to her chest. "I didn't…" She couldn't draw in a decent breath. The branches outside the floor-to-ceiling windows bent in the wind. Suddenly, Nicole felt very claustrophobic. Dizzy.

"I didn't steal the jewelry." She finally spit out the words. Her pulse thrummed in her ears.

Brett stood and placed a hand on the small of Nicole's back. "Mrs. Peters, you should consider the possibility that Nicole is telling the truth."

"I'm a pretty good judge of character." Mrs. Peters lifted her chin, a regal gesture diminished slightly by the nurse wrapping a blood pressure cuff around her thin arm. "And I expect you will not let your bias interfere when it comes to investigating the thief. The *true* thief."

Nicole watched the needle on the blood pressure cuff and wondered what her own blood pressure was now. Her face was on fire.

Mrs. Peters opened her mouth to say something else and she started to cough again.

The nurse stepped forward this time. "I'm sorry, you really have to go."

Nicole nodded, feeling utterly defeated. Brett led Nicole outside. She turned and studied the Peterses' home, a fancy home by anyone's standards. "I could never relate to people who come from such wealth. Maybe she looks at me, knows where I came from, and automatically thinks I'm dishonest."

"Prejudice comes in many forms."

"Do you really believe I'm innocent?"

"I told you I did." A flash of something sparked in Brett's eyes.

Nicole closed her eyes briefly. "You reassured Mrs. Peters that you would fully investigate the crime, making me think you're still going to investigate me."

Brett descended the porch steps, then turned to look up at her. "I have to do my job regardless of my personal feelings."

Fear and anger and disappointment twisted around Nicole's heart. If Brett had intended to reassure her, he had failed miserably.

"You told him, didn't you?" Gigi pointed the remote at the television and turned down the volume.

A flush of dread washed over Nicole. She felt as though she was about fifteen and being scolded. And she wasn't in any mood after her disastrous meeting with Mrs. Peters this morning. How would she ever prove her innocence?

Nicole grabbed the fleece blanket from the back of the couch and threw it over her shoulders. She wasn't used to sitting around the house watching afternoon soaps, but if she was going to do it, she may as well embrace the experience.

Nicole sighed heavily. "Brett had a right to know about Ethan."

"Ethan's father was the only man who had a right to know. And we all know how Max took the news."

Nicole's stomach bottomed out. "Gigi, don't be so cruel. The man is dead. God rest his soul."

Gigi bowed her head for the slightest of moments, as if she suddenly felt contrite for her comment. "I'm sorry. I worry…. And now you're out of a job."

"I'm hoping it's temporary." Nicole forced a lightness to her tone she didn't feel.

"The Peters have to realize you'd never steal from anyone."

Tears pricked the backs of Nicole's eyes. Gigi was the one person who had always provided unconditional love.

Gigi's lips flattened into a thin line. "I'm sorry I made you come back to Silver Lake. I know you're not happy here."

"I'm happy."

Her grandmother angled her head to study her. "I appreciate the effort, but I can tell when you're not happy. Tell me, is Brett a good man?"

Nicole wanted to say, "Yes," but the word got lodged in her throat. She feared he hadn't embraced her innocence, but could she blame him?

Instead, Nicole said, "Ethan needs a father figure. Who better than his uncle?"

Gigi lifted her chin slightly. "He has us. Two strong women." She shook her head. "Men are highly overrated. Your mother relied on men to solve her problems." She laughed, a brittle sound. "Look how that worked out for her. She lost custody of you and she died alone, her drugs more important than her family." Gigi's even, cold tone sent ice shooting through Nicole's veins.

Nicole scooted off the couch, knelt next to her grandmother's wheelchair and pulled the older woman's callused hand into her own. "I'm sorry you've had so much hurt in your life." Gigi squeezed her hand, but didn't say anything. "I try not to think of the bad stuff. The memory I hold close is when Mom and I would crawl into my bed and cuddle. I'd drift off to sleep, the smell of Dove soap in my nose."

Gigi twirled a strand of Nicole's hair around her fingers. "You certainly have selective memory."

Nicole touched her grandmother's knee. "I remember

the other stuff, too, but it's easier to love Mom when I only think of the good."

Gigi shifted her unfocused gaze toward the twenty-year-old television set.

"Brett *is a* good man." He was. "He's different than his brother," Nicole said, her voice soft, encouraging.

A slow smile graced her grandmother's face. "You've fallen for him."

Denial immediately sprang to mind but died on her lips. "He's watching out for us, Gigi. He's good for Ethan."

Gigi shook her head. "We don't need watching out for."

Nicole didn't want to worry her grandmother, but she wanted to keep everyone safe. "There's some weird stuff—"

"What are you talking about? Weird stuff?"

Nicole slipped away from Gigi and sat on the couch. She pulled the blanket in tight around her middle. "The man I put in prison is out. He works at the cemetery and was talking to Ethan at Missy's funeral. I'm afraid he wants to get back at me for testifying against him."

"Are you okay?"

"I'm fine. But Brett is investigating a few things. He's going to make sure everything stays that way."

Gigi studied Nicole's face for a long minute and something flickered behind her eyes. Her features seemed to soften, as if she had come to some conclusion.

Nicole stood and gave the older woman a kiss on her forehead, the familiar scent of her floral perfume tickling her senses, making Nicole feel both protected and nostalgic at the same time. "Until we figure out what's going on, I need you to keep the doors locked. Don't answer the door if you're not expecting anyone. And we can't let Ethan out of our sight until Brett gets enough evidence to arrest Richard White, the man I had put in prison."

Gigi clutched the arms of her wheelchair. "What good am I? In this wheelchair?"

Nicole understood her grandmother's frustration, fearing she wouldn't be able to protect the family she loved because she couldn't walk. Nicole stood and wrapped her arms around her grandmother.

"You are my rock."

When Nicole pulled away, she saw tears in her grandmother's eyes. "I wish I could have done more for you when you were growing up. It pained me when you started down the same path as your mother." Gigi shook her head. "I wish you never had to run away from Silver Lake."

"You gave me a home. Unconditional love. The bad choices I made were my own." Nicole patted her grandmother's shoulder. "I'm not going anywhere now. I promise."

Out of the corner of her eye she could see the opening credits for her grandmother's favorite afternoon soap. "Your show's starting." Nicole slipped the remote from her grandmother's hand and turned the TV volume up. "Don't worry. Brett's a good guy. He's helping me."

Nicole had to have faith.

Gigi brushed her thumb across Nicole's cheek. "You are a smart girl. Be safe." Nicole sensed her grandmother meant that in more ways than one.

The rumble of the bus drew Nicole's attention. She rushed to the front door and opened it. The glass storm door immediately fogged up. It was freezing outside. The lights on the bus flashed red. For some reason, Nicole held her breath until she saw Ethan appear at the open door of the bus. With slumped shoulders, he plodded up the driveway, kicking his feet as he walked.

She pushed the door open for him and her stomach dropped. Gone was her usually happy, chatty son. "What's wrong?"

Ethan's lips trembled as he fought to hold back the tears. The strings to her heart tugged when she realized he was afraid to reveal his emotions in front of her.

"Nothing," he said in a voice that sounded far from being nothing.

"Did something happen at school?" Nicole tried to unzip his jacket, but he stepped out of reach.

"I'm not a baby."

A mixture of anger and compassion squeezed her heart. "Ethan, what's wrong?"

"Nothing, Mom. I said nothing." He spat out the words. "Stop being a pest."

Nicole straightened and jammed her fists onto her hips. "It seems you've had a rough day, but that doesn't give you the right to talk to me like that, young man."

Ethan's face crumbled. He toed off his boots and one of them hit the wall, leaving a slushy mess. He opened his mouth, perhaps to apologize, but instead he ran to his room and slammed the door.

Nicole rolled her shoulders and prayed for patience.

Brett stepped into the grand foyer of his parents' house. He had grown up here, but it never felt quite like home. His mother had worried her two sons would stain the carpet or break her precious antiques or unfluff her fancy pillows.

The clacking of heels on marble put his nerves on edge. His mother appeared, dressed impeccably, as if she were expecting company and not her only son. "*He's* in the carriage house. Maybe you can convince him to come in. It has to be freezing out there."

Brett gave his mother a perfunctory kiss on the cheek.

"So, what did the doctors say at Father's visit?" Brett tugged off his leather gloves and stuffed them into his jacket pocket. His pulse ratcheted up in his ears as he waited for the details of the dreadful news.

"The cancer has spread." She rearranged her features to hide any emotion. Another son would pull his mother into a hug, but they didn't have a traditional relationship. There was a wall between them. His mother had claimed more than once that she didn't have the mother gene.

Brett gave his mother a slight nod. "I'm sorry. Are you okay?" He took a step toward her and she lifted her hand, blocking his approach.

"I'm fine." Her stiff posture said she was anything but fine. "He's refusing further treatment."

Brett stopped midstride. "I'll talk to him."

The coolness he felt from his mother matched the brisk winter night. Brett zipped up his jacket and crossed the snow-covered yard, his boots crunching on the thin layer of ice coating the snow. The light from the carriage house glowed brightly. His father had always come here to work out his problems. Problems that usually involved rich clients who had gotten themselves into a legal mess or a son who had gotten involved with drugs.

Brett had spent his entire childhood trying to make his father proud. Becoming the chief of police had been an achievement, but it was not exactly the career his parents had wanted for their only surviving son.

Brett opened the door and stepped over the lip into the carriage house. The rich smell of wood hung in the air. His father had on a mask and was bent over the hull of a cedar rowboat. He ran the sandpaper in straight lines.

Swoosh. Swoosh. Swoosh.

Brett stood for a moment watching. His father had grown thinner since the last time he had seen him. He'd always been an imposing figure in Brett's life. In everyone's life. No one messed with Brett Maxwell Eggert, Esquire.

Not even his sons.

"Did your mother send you?" His father continued working on his project.

Swoosh. Swoosh. Swoosh.

"You had a doctor's appointment today."

"I know. I was there."

Swoosh. Swoosh. Swoosh.

"Dad…" The single word sounded foreign on his lips. It was usually sir or father.

"Mother said you're refusing any more treatment."

His father tossed his tool and lifted the mask from his face, his expression shuttered. He had traded one mask for another. Brett had never been able to read the man, except for his anger.

"I want to live the rest of my life on my terms."

"Yes, sir." The whisper of a familiar prayer floated across Brett's brain, then disappeared. Maybe he had been wrong to abandon his faith. Because sometimes faith was all a person had.

His father took a step toward him. "You're not going to change my mind."

Shaking his head, his father picked up the sanding tool and resumed his work. Brett was about to turn to leave, when his father stopped working and looked up again.

"I miss him."

Brett studied his father a minute, letting the words sink in. His father missed *him. Max.*

"I do, too. I wish things could have been different." A thought settled in his gut and made Brett uneasy. If his father's diagnosis was as dire as Brett was led to believe, soon his father would join Max. Was the promise of eternal life with his son behind his father's decision to refuse further treatment? Despite his father's love of all things material, faith had been a big part of his family's life.

Brett was the only one who had lost faith after Max's death.

His father walked slowly over to a stool in the corner

of the garage. He sat down, the gesture so deliberate Brett could see the pain in every movement.

"I should have been there for you boys more when you were growing up."

Brett cleared his throat, afraid he wouldn't be able to speak around the lump in his throat. Like his mother, his father was rarely demonstrative. "You did what you had to do."

"I thought it was important. To work. To have a big career. To feel important." His father drew in a shaky breath. "I made a lot of money." He wiped his forehead with his shirtsleeve. "I'm afraid I won't have pockets in my shroud to take it with me."

Brett chuckled, despite the pain in his heart.

His father pushed to his feet. "I've been working on this boat since you and Max were boys."

"I remember." More times than not, if his father was home, he was either in his office working or out here. Working.

The lost expression in his father's eyes knocked Brett off kilter. "I've never once been out in this rowboat," his father muttered. His words dripped with regret.

Brett's phone rang, breaking the mood. His father's shoulders sagged and he pointed at Brett. "I suppose you better get that. It might be work."

Brett stared at him for a second. "Yeah." He unclipped the phone from his belt and answered it. The caller ID indicated Nicole's home phone.

"Hello."

A small child sobbed over the line.

NINE

A loud rapping sounded at the front door. Nicole started. She had been dozing on the couch in front of the television. She touched Gigi's shoulder as she passed. "It's okay. I'll get it."

She pulled back the sheer curtain covering the window on the front door. Brett stood, fist poised to knock again, his mouth tightened in concern. Her stomach twisted. Something was wrong. Very wrong.

She undid the bolts and yanked the door open. "What's wrong?" She felt as if she had been asking that a lot lately.

"Ethan called me. He's upset. I could hardly make out what he was saying." Brett's eyes darted around the small space. "Where is he?"

Nicole strode toward Ethan's bedroom, her pulse pounding in her ears. Brett followed. "Ethan's in his room. He came home from school in a grumpy mood. He came out to eat dinner and hardly said anything, then went right back to his room on his own. He wouldn't tell me why he was upset. I thought he was just overtired. Kids get that way, you know? He was trying my patience. I have no idea why he'd call you. I'm sorry." The words poured from her lips as she replayed every little detail of the afternoon in her mind.

She turned the handle on his door and found it locked. "Ethan." She jiggled the handle, anger and a growing sense of unease prickling the hair at the back of her neck. "Ethan, open the door right now or you are in big trouble."

Silence.

Brett reached around her and tried the handle. "Ethan, it's Chief Eggert. Open the door."

Rustling sounded from the other side of the door. Nicole let out a relieved rush of air.

Through the crack in the door, Nicole could see Ethan's tear-stained face. She pushed open the door and Ethan bolted to his bed and buried his face in his pillow. Her heart went out to her little man. "Something must have happened at school. I really just thought he was overtired."

Nicole sat on the edge of the bed. She rubbed Ethan's back in small circles. She had spent countless hours doing this when he was little to lull him to sleep. The days when Mommy made everything better. "You can tell me anything, Ethan. Please." Nicole hated the desperation in her voice. She hated the helplessness she felt when it came to her son.

A solid hand squeezed her shoulder. She lifted her face to see Brett's compassionate eyes watching her. "Can I talk to him?"

Nicole hesitated a moment. She nodded, stood and walked out into the hallway. Her son had asked for Brett. Not her. A little dagger pierced her heart. Weren't moms supposed to be the center of a seven-year-old's universe? She paced outside the door. She knew in her heart, she shouldn't eavesdrop, but she had to know what was going on with her little man.

Brett's boots sounded on the hardwood floor. The bed creaked. Nicole flattened herself against the wall and tipped her head back, imagining Brett sitting on the corner of the bed. The spot where she had sat only moments ago.

"What's up, buddy?" Brett asked, his voice deep and soothing.

Nicole covered her mouth with the tips of her fingers.

"Kids at school still bothering you?"

Still? The back of her throat ached. Why hadn't Ethan told her about troubles at school?

She could hear Ethan sniffling. She couldn't hear what he was muttering, then it became clearer. "A kid said my mom was a thief."

Nicole's heart raced, nearly drowning out all other sounds. She bit her lip, trying to tamp down a yelp of denial.

"Why would a kid at school say that?"

"He said his grandma was buried last month and her jewelry went missing. He heard his parents talking. Is it true? Is that why Mommy's home now when I get off the bus? Did she lose her job because she stole something?" The pleading in her son's voice broke her heart. She forced herself to stay rooted in place, knowing Ethan would feel betrayed if he knew she was listening. Nicole sucked in a breath and waited for Brett's answer.

"Do you think it's true?" Brett's voice sounded calm, reassuring.

Ethan hiccupped. Nicole wished she could see his face. "My mom taught me about the ten commandments. The third one says you shouldn't steal."

"I don't think you mean the third commandment," Brett hesitated, "but you have the right idea. You shouldn't steal."

"That's right." Ethan's voice sounded brighter. "My mom told me not to worry so much with the numbers because that makes it harder to learn, but she told me I should understand that God wants us to be good people. To make the right choices."

"Your mom's a good person." Nicole imagined Brett holding her son's hand. His nephew's hand.

Silence stretched across the small space. The clock ticked on the wall. Laugh tracks sounded from the TV program her grandmother was watching.

"My friend's lying," Ethan said, his voice soft.

"Your friend might be repeating something he heard in his home. But I'm confident his parents are mistaken. Your mother wouldn't take anything that wasn't hers."

Something banged against the wall. Nicole knew that sometimes Ethan hit his elbow on the wall when he was adjusting the pillows behind his head. "I know." Ethan's voice sounded very small.

"Cut your buddy some slack. Eventually he'll realize he's only repeating rumors."

"What are rumors?"

"It's when someone repeats something they hear whether or not they know it's true." Brett's voice grew softer. "And it's never a good idea to repeat bad stuff about anyone, right?"

"Yes." Ethan sniffed. "I wish I had more friends."

"I think you need to talk to your mom about this. Tell her what's worrying you."

"I can't."

"Why not?" Brett was doing great, keeping his tone light.

Nicole leaned against the wall and she pressed a hand to her throat. Brett had won another piece of her heart.

She was in big trouble.

"My mom has enough going on. She lost her friend." Ethan's voice quivered. "She's worried all the time. I wish I was bigger and could help my mom."

Nicole pinched her lips between her fingers to keep quiet. A part of her wished she hadn't listened. *That's what you get.*

Sucking in a breath, she crept down the hall, trying not to make a sound. Suddenly her grandmother's house seemed very small. The walls pushed in on her. She kept walking to the front door. She stuffed her feet into her boots and her arms into her thick winter jacket. She unlocked the door and stepped out onto the snowy porch.

She flipped up her hood to stop the cold breeze from drifting down her neck. She pulled her mittens out of her pocket and put them on. She marched down the front walk, now covered in a few inches of freshly fallen snow. The shovel was propped against the garage. She grabbed it and started shoveling.

The straight, even lines kept her focused. The smooth zing of the metal scraping against the black asphalt gave her some small sense of satisfaction. When her entire world was spiraling out of control, she could control this. Straight lines in the snow.

Snow, take that!

Nicole didn't realize she was crying until sharp pinpricks of icy pain cut her cheeks. She flung the snow and stabbed the shovel into a small pile of snow. She ran her damp pink mitten across her cheek.

Lord, please guide me through this. I know I made some really, really dumb decisions in the past. But I'm making good decisions now. Please help others see I am not who I used to be. Please protect my sweet son's heart.

"Nicole."

She spun around at the sound of Brett's deep voice. Clearing her throat, she reached back to grab the shovel by its red handle. "The snow keeps coming, doesn't it?" She scraped the snow in neat lines again, once having to go around Brett. Her skin prickled, aware that he was watching her. She stopped and rested her elbow on the handle of the shovel, trying to act casual. "Is Ethan okay?"

"You were listening."

Nicole opened her mouth to protest, then decided lying—even a little white one—wasn't such a good idea. Especially after pleading with God to help her stay on the right path.

Nicole nodded.

Brett took a step closer. They weren't touching, but the heat radiating from him warmed her. "You remember how kids are. They can be mean."

She nodded, grief clogging her throat.

"You should talk to Ethan. Reassure him that everything is going to be all right."

She met his gaze. "Is it?"

Brett cupped her chin, forcing her to meet his gaze. "I'm here for you." He leaned forward and brushed his warm lips across hers. Her heart expanded.

The rumble of a snowplow barreling down the narrow country road drew her attention. She stepped away from Brett, a shy smile on her lips. "Snow's starting to come down pretty heavy. Sorry if Ethan called you away from work."

"He didn't. I was visiting my parents."

Nicole's heart sank. "Oh." His parents would never accept her in their lives. Another reason she and Brett could never be together.

It was only a kiss.

He ran his hand down the sleeve of her coat. Big snowflakes landed on his hair, then melted. His nose had gotten red from the chilly temperatures. "They're really not bad people. They're hurting."

Nicole lifted her eyebrows, but didn't say anything.

"My dad's not doing well." Brett took the shovel from her hand, his leather glove brushing against her sopping wet mitten.

"Oh." She mentally scolded herself. She wasn't being very articulate.

"His cancer spread and he's refusing further treatment." Brett stopped shoveling and propped the shovel in the snow pile much like she had done.

"I'm sorry."

Brett gave her a strange look. "My father never recovered from losing Max."

The ache intensified in Nicole's throat.

"I need a favor, Nicole. And before you say no, I need you to consider it. Really consider it."

"What?" Her breath formed a white cloud and disappeared.

"I want my father to meet his grandson before he dies."

Brett crouched down behind the red plastic sled. "Climb on, buddy. I got it." Brett squinted against the sun reflecting off the snow.

Ethan lumbered around the side of the sled in his blue boots and black snowsuit. A red scarf covered his nose and mouth, but Brett detected a smile in the young boy's eyes. "I want Mom to go down the hill with me again."

"Again?" Nicole's groan didn't match the smile on her pink lips.

"One more time," Ethan pleaded.

Nicole brushed past Brett and lifted an eyebrow. "Don't let go of the sled until I get all the way on. I don't want to go barreling down the hill on my backside."

"Don't be such a worrier." Brett playfully tugged a strand of the long brown hair flowing out from under Nicole's cute knit cap. "Get in."

She lifted an eyebrow as if to say that he'd better not be messing with her. She straddled the sled behind Ethan. Brett caught a hint of her cucumber shampoo while she settled in.

She glanced up at Brett, the setting sun sparkling in her bright eyes. "I can't remember the last time I went sledding." She wrapped one arm around her son and pulled him tight. She gripped the sled handle with her other hand. "I don't know about this. And don't push us too hard. I don't want to end up in the ditch."

Brett squeezed her shoulder. "You'll be fine."

"Ready!" Ethan shouted, staring straight ahead, his little hands firmly wrapped around the edges of the sled.

Brett gave them a little push and stood. He watched them bounce down the hill. They missed a divot and came to a smooth stop near the bottom of the hill. Mother and son had their heads tilted back in laughter.

Something inside him warmed despite the temperature. Could he be falling for Nicole? It seemed wrong, yet right.

He was eager to tell Ethan he was his uncle. Nicole promised they'd tell him over hot chocolate back at the house.

The pair climbed the hill while Brett waited on top. Nicole's breath came out in labored puffs. She narrowed her gaze at Brett, but he could tell she wasn't mad. He saw the twinkle in her eye. "How come I have to do all the work, going up and down the hill?" She gestured back down the hill. "I'm out of shape."

He bit back the first comment that sprang to mind. Nicole was definitely not out of shape. Brett swiped at a snowflake that had landed on Nicole's eyebrow. "I don't think a chairlift is in the town's budget."

Nicole shoved the sled into Brett's chest. "*You* go down with Ethan. I'll push."

Brett grabbed the sled and turned it over in his hands. "I don't think that thing would hold me. I'd hate to snap it in half."

Nicole leaned in closer. "Chicken." She stuffed her mittens under her armpits and flapped. "Bawk, bawk, bawk."

Brett shook his head and laughed. "I don't succumb to peer pressure."

"Fuddy-duddy." She lifted an eyebrow, taunting him.

"Can I go down by myself?" Ethan took the sled and lined it up on the hill. "Please?" Without waiting for an answer, he sat and pushed off with fisted gloves.

"Be careful," Nicole hollered one last warning as her son picked up momentum gliding down the hill. Brett heard Nicole suck in a gasp when her son hit a bump. His arms and legs went flying before he landed awkwardly on the hard-packed snow. The sled kept going without its passenger.

Before either he or Nicole had a chance to react, Ethan sprang up and waved his arms in the air. "I'm okay." He brushed off his arms and snow pants. "It's all good."

Nicole lifted her mittens to her cheeks. "That kid is going to be the death of me." She headed down the hill and Brett followed.

"Boys will be boys." Brett watched Ethan run after the sled. "Max used to be a daredevil when he was a little kid. I spent my entire childhood keeping him out of trouble."

Brett forced a smile as he realized what he had just said. The sled had come to a rest in the ditch alongside the country road. Brett cupped his hands around his mouth and yelled, "Leave the sled, I'll get it."

But Ethan either didn't hear him or chose to ignore him. The little boy's arms and legs pumped as he ran across the field toward the ditch. Nicole and Brett ran down the hill. Nicole lost her footing and Brett grabbed her arm, preventing her from landing on her backside.

"Whoa." Nicole regained her footing and kept running. "Ethan, stop. Leave the sled. Don't go near that ditch."

Brett picked up his pace. "I'll stop him."

"Ethan!" Nicole hollered when Ethan scooted down the edge of the ditch.

Brett caught up with Ethan and grabbed his arm, pulling him and the sled out of the ditch. "Careful."

Nicole caught up, breathing heavily, a look of fright in her eyes. "What were you thinking? I yelled for you to stop."

"I was only getting my sled." Ethan jutted his jaw in defiance. "You worry too much."

Nicole leaned down in front of him and clutched his arms. "I'm your mother, it's my job to worry." Ethan bowed his head in contrition. She nudged his chin, forcing him to look at her. "And Chief Eggert worries too."

"Why would Chief Eggert worry so much about me?" Ethan sulked because he had been scolded.

Brett locked eyes with Nicole. He detected a subtle nod. "There's something very important we want to tell you," she said in a soft voice.

Brett's pulse kicked up a notch.

"Chief Eggert…Brett is your uncle."

Brett smiled and cupped Ethan's shoulder. "Your daddy was my little brother."

A wide smile spread across Ethan's face. "Really?"

Nicole kissed Ethan's forehead. "Really."

Ethan smiled up at Brett. "So does that mean I can call you Uncle Brett?"

Brett's heart warmed. "Absolutely, buddy."

His nephew wrapped his arms around Brett's waist. A contentedness filled his soul.

TEN

Nicole made Ethan hot chocolate and they settled in front of the fireplace. Her body ached from a day of sledding. Gigi was content knitting, something Nicole hadn't seen her do in a while. Music played quietly in the background.

Nicole pulled back the curtain to see if she could see Brett in the yard. He had insisted on putting the sled away in the shed when it would have been perfectly fine resting against the side of the house. The shed door yawned open, but there was no sign of him.

She had spontaneously told Ethan about his uncle while they were sledding. It seemed like the right thing at the right time. Butterflies flitted in her stomach. Now there was no going back.

"Is something wrong, Mom?" Nicole cupped Ethan's cheek; his trusting eyes searched hers. The chocolate mustache on his wind-chapped face made her smile.

She shook her head. "I thought Uncle Brett would be back in already." Nicole pulled back the curtain again and this time she saw Brett talking on his phone outside the shed. He paced back and forth as if something was bothering him. Her throat tightened. Maybe he had news about whoever ran Missy off the road. The familiar guilt nagged at her. *She* was supposed to have been in that car. *She* was the one who was supposed to be dead. Buried in the same cemetery as Ethan's father.

She worked her lower lip. Perhaps it was best to make the Eggert family a part of Ethan's life. Ethan would have no one if she died. Gigi wasn't getting any younger. Her emotions swung between apprehension and excitement. Her son did need a male role model.

"What's Uncle Brett doing out there?" Ethan turned away from the window and carried his hot chocolate over to the couch and sat. He picked the spoon out of the mug and licked off the whipped cream. "He looks mad."

She tucked her chin in and forced a bright smile despite her nerves. "Why do you say that?" She found herself watching Brett. Late-afternoon shadows on his features made his expression difficult to read.

"He just does."

She scooted around the coffee table and sat on the edge so she could look her son squarely in the eyes. "How are you doing with the news that Brett is your uncle?" Apprehension pushed in on her, making it difficult to breathe.

"It's awesome. Now he can come over more and hang out with me." Ethan leaned around Nicole so he could see Gigi. "Mind if I change the channel?"

"Go ahead." Gigi lifted her knitting.

Nicole smiled at Gigi. It broke Nicole's heart to see how much Gigi had aged in the years Nicole had stayed away from Silver Lake. Once again, guilt made her restless. She was tired of feeling guilty. She paced next to the window. "I wonder what's taking Brett so long."

The side door opened and Nicole sucked in a breath. A moment later, Brett walked in, a somber expression on his face. Nicole wished she knew him well enough to read what was going on behind his eyes. Something about his expression made her even more uneasy.

"Everything okay?" Nicole asked.

Brett seemed to shake himself.

"You were talking on the phone a long time out there."

"Oh, yeah." Brett seemed very distracted. "Work stuff."

Nicole lifted the remote and clicked off the television,

sending the room into silence. She tossed the remote on the couch. "Anything you can share?"

Brett smiled at Ethan. "I have to head out, but I'll see you soon." He avoided her question.

"Okay." Ethan sounded deflated.

Brett stepped into the room and sat on the arm of the couch. "I was thrilled to find out I was your uncle."

Ethan scooted toward the edge of the couch cushion. "Me, too…I mean, that I'm your nephew."

Gigi smiled and put her knitting needles down in her lap. "The old lady has some competition."

Ethan stood and wrapped his arms around his great-grandmother. "I love you, Gigi." Nicole's heart expanded and she nearly burst with pride.

Gigi patted Ethan's back. "You're a good kid."

Ethan stood straight. "Uncle Brett, I hope we get to spend more time together."

"Absolutely, but I have to run now." Brett playfully mussed up his nephew's hair.

"Don't you have time for hot chocolate?" Nicole studied Brett's face. Something had happened between the time they had arrived home from sledding and now.

"I'm sorry I really have to go." Brett rubbed Ethan's arm. "I'll call your mom later and we'll make plans."

"Of course." She feigned a cheery tone. Something was off. "Ethan, stay here and drink your hot chocolate. I'm going to walk Uncle Brett out."

Ethan used his spoon to scoop up the whipped cream floating on top of his hot chocolate.

Nicole followed Brett to the front door. In a hushed voice, she asked Brett if everything was okay. "You seem distant after you put the sled away in the shed."

"Why didn't you want me to go into the shed?"

Nicole narrowed her gaze at him. "What are you talking about?"

"Was there something in the shed you didn't want me to see?" Lines formed around the tight set of his mouth.

Nicole jerked her head back. "I'm confused."

Brett reached into his pocket and pulled out a bag of jewelry. Nicole stared at him, color rising in her cheeks. "What is that?"

"I found it in *your* shed."

She blinked back her shock. "More jewelry.…"

"Yes. It was sitting on the log pile in the shed."

Nicole slowly shook her head. "You don't think I put it there, do you? Left it out in the open?" Her pulse thrummed in her ears as her mind raced. "How stupid would that be?"

"You didn't want me to go into the shed."

"Because it was too much trouble, that's all." Exasperation and defeat lay heavy on her chest. Would she and Brett forever go round and round about her innocence?

Brett stared at her with an unreadable expression. "I agree. It's too convenient. If this White guy is trying to cause trouble for you, what better way than to put something out in the open."

Nicole crossed her arms tight over her midsection. "He'd have to be watching us. Know that we went sledding. That you might go in the shed."

Brett nodded slowly. This time concern was evident on his face. "Lock the doors up tight when I leave. I just got off the phone with Mr. White's parole officer. The two of us are going to pay another visit to Mr. White right now."

The next morning Brett stepped into the lobby of the funeral home. A lamp burned brightly on an end table by a single chair. The place had a lonely quality. Creepy almost.

Derreck poked his head out of his office door. "Come on in." Brett had called ahead to schedule a meeting.

Brett crossed the room and sat in front of Derreck's desk. "Thanks for meeting with me on such short notice."

"We had an early morning call. Family wants a viewing tomorrow. There's no such thing as nine-to-five in the funeral home business." Derreck sat behind the large mahogany desk and tapped the pads of his fingers together. Brett imagined this was his how-can-I-help-you-now-that-your-loved-one-is-gone pose. Something about it gave Brett the willies.

How did someone do this for a living? Brett supposed many people would question *his* sanity for choosing to be a police officer when he could have easily followed his father's footsteps into his lucrative law practice.

Brett leaned forward and reached into his pocket. A knot hardened in his gut. He pulled out the small bag of jewelry. It was against protocol, but Brett wanted to be told there was absolutely no way Nicole could have stolen this jewelry. He wanted to clear her name. Brett hoped Derreck would tell him that the jewelry—at least some of it—came from bodies that predated Nicole's employment, proving that she was as innocent as she claimed to be.

Nicole wasn't the only one with trust issues.

A bemused expression settled on Derreck's ruddy features. "This is the second time you've strolled in here with jewelry." He tipped his head. "These pieces came from the dearly departed, too?"

"Do you recognize them?" Brett kept his expression neutral as he fingered the jewelry through the clear plastic bag.

Derreck lifted his index finger in a hold-on-a-minute gesture. He picked up the phone, pressed a couple of numbers and waited. "Come up here a sec," he said into the phone.

Derreck hung up the phone. "Gene's downstairs. He

handles most of the bodies. If the jewelry belonged to any of them, he'll recognize it."

A minute later, Brett heard shuffling steps on stairs, then over the carpet. Brett shifted in his seat and saw Gene lurking in the doorway. He had on a white lab coat and a somber expression. He didn't say anything.

Derreck offered the bag to Gene. "You recognize this jewelry?"

Gene leaned over and inspected the contents of the bag without touching it. "Yes, I do."

"From recently deceased?" Derreck tipped his head, never taking his eyes off Gene.

"Yep." Gene leaned in closer and poked at the bag with his index finger. "I'd say all within the past four to six months. I could double check the files. Mr. Peters always makes notes when someone wants to be buried with jewelry. He encourages the family to keep the jewelry to remember their loved ones." Gene's lips thinned. "But I suppose people don't need things to remember people they love."

"Thanks, Gene," Derreck cut in, stopping the man from rambling.

Brett's heart sank. Nicole had worked at the funeral home during the thefts. He ran a hand over his chin. Whoever wanted to frame her was doing a good job.

A whisper of doubt crept into his brain: had Nicole lied to him like his brother had? Max had claimed he was done with drugs only to die in a crash while under the influence.

"Why do you have this?" Gene stared at the jewelry, now sitting on the corner of Derreck's desk. "The family requested their loved ones be buried with the jewelry."

"That's what I'm trying to figure out here, Gene." Derreck's tone was much like that of a parent scolding a child. "Do you have any ideas?"

Gene shook his head adamantly; he snuck a look at

Brett, then studied his feet. "No, I don't." He tapped the leg of the desk with his shoe. "Anything else? I want to finish up here. I don't like to leave work hanging over my head."

Derreck shook his head. "We're all set."

Brett waited until he heard the click of the basement door. A muscle ticked in his jaw. "Can you get me a list of the recently deceased and when they were buried?" He wanted to compare it to the dates of Nicole's employment. If he could find one stolen piece that predated her employment…

"Sure." Derreck stood up. "Anything else? I have work to do."

Brett ran his hand along his jaw. "And to reiterate. The back door is rarely locked?"

Anger flashed briefly in Derreck's eyes. "I wouldn't say rarely, but we do leave it open for deliveries. Silver Lake is a pretty quiet town."

"You might want to change that practice." If someone like Richard White had snuck into the funeral home, he was pretty stealthy. How many break-ins would it take to accumulate that much jewelry?

When Brett and the parole officer had paid White a visit after the shed incident, White reluctantly gave them names of friends who provided him with an alibi for most of yesterday. So much for Brett's theory that White tossed the jewelry onto the woodpile in the shed, hoping it would be discovered when they returned with the sled. However, his friends weren't exactly model citizens.

"Where did you find this jewelry?" Derreck asked, snapping Brett out of his musings.

Brett hesitated for a minute. "At Nicole's residence."

Derreck angled his head as if to say, "Oh, really?"

Brett held up his hand. "I don't believe she stole the jewelry. I think someone is setting her up."

Derreck seemed to consider this a moment. "Are you sure you're not too close to the case?"

"I'm doing my job."

"Make sure you are. I'm going to want an arrest on this." Derreck pushed his thick, black plastic glasses up on his nose. "It's bad for business. And business is already bad enough."

ELEVEN

Nicole sang the closing hymn while Ethan pushed on her hip, anxious to spill out into the church aisle and go home. She bestowed on him her best knock-it-off look and went back to singing. The church service was beautiful, but Nicole had failed to focus solely on the reason she was here. She couldn't stop thinking about the stolen jewelry found in her shed. Someone was determined to make trouble for her and she prayed Brett really did believe her when she said she had nothing to do with it.

She tilted her face toward the church's stained-glass windows and said one final prayer for peace. Whatever evil was going on around her, pulling her down, she wanted it over. She wanted to go back to her boring day-to-day life caring for her son and grandmother in small town Silver Lake.

She sniffed. She doubted that would ever be possible.

The choir held the last note and Nicole turned to leave, reaching behind her for Ethan's hand. She stopped abruptly. Brett walked slowly up the aisle toward her.

Ethan tugged her hand and made clear his displeasure at having to stay in his church pew. Embarrassment heated her cheeks. She'd have to give her son a refresher course on the proper behavior in church.

"Morning," Brett said, a slow smile forming on his lips. A smile that warmed her heart. Then he looked down at Ethan. "How are you doing, buddy?"

"Good." Ethan beamed up at his uncle. "Are you coming over today?"

"I have to talk to your mom first, okay?" Brett placed his hand on Ethan's shoulder. "Can you wait here a second?"

"Sure." Ethan sat on the bench, quite amiably considering how eager he had been to leave a second ago.

Brett took Nicole's hand and led her a few feet away.

"I thought you didn't go to church." Nicole studied his face, something unreadable flickered across his features.

Brett lifted his palm casually. "My mother asked me to come with her…and I suppose I have a lot to be grateful for." His gaze drifted to Ethan.

"Listen…" He leaned in close, the scent of his clean aftershave tickling her nose. "I hate to spring this on you, but I thought now would be a good time to introduce Ethan to my mom."

Nicole's stomach dropped to her shoes and she couldn't form any words.

Brett kept his voice low so as not to be overheard. "I understand if you're not ready."

Nicole drew in a deep breath, a burst of courage filling her lungs. There would never be a good time, so why not now? If they waited, they risked everyone finding out through the rumor mill. She nodded and squeaked out the word, "Okay."

He tilted his head to study her face. "Are you sure?"

"Let's do this." Nicole turned around and reached out for Ethan's hand. "Ethan, Uncle Brett's mom is at church this morning. Your grandmother."

Her son's eyebrows shot up, but he didn't say anything.

Brett slipped in next to him on the church bench. "Would you like to meet her?"

Ethan shrugged as if the idea was too much to take in.

Nicole tipped her head toward the entrance. "Come on. I'm sure she'll be thrilled to meet you."

Nicole held Ethan's hand as they walked down the aisle.

Her pulse raced in her ears muffling the clack, clack, clack of her shoes on the marble floor. She had dreaded this moment since she first laid eyes on her beautiful son.

Mrs. Eggert was standing in the foyer of the church, her silver hair wound tightly in a bun at the base of her neck. She finished her conversation with another woman and turned to face them.

"Hello, Mother," Brett said.

"Hello," came her crisp reply.

"Good morning. Beautiful church service." Nicole tossed out the standard pleasantries after Sunday worship, realizing how silly small talk was.

"Yes. Yes it was." Mrs. Eggert's voice sounded sweet as molasses. The syrupy sound sent irrational terror oozing into Nicole's heart. She wiped her sweat-slicked palm on her khaki pants.

"How are you, young man?" Mrs. Eggert touched Ethan's arm and smiled.

Oh, I'm not ready to share my son with this woman.

Guilt niggled her insides. Nicole was standing in a house of God while refusing to forgive her son's grandma. To welcome her into her lives.

"I'm fine." Ethan's eyebrows smooshed together and he frowned.

Awkward silence stretched between them. The chatter of the congregation filing out of the church around them sounded distant, distorted. Nicole drew in a deep breath. "Mrs. Eggert—"

Brett held out his hand, stopping Nicole. "Mom, I'd like you to meet Ethan, Max's son. Your grandson."

Mrs. Eggert's hand flew to her chest and her eyes filled with unshed tears. "Max's son?" Her gaze drifted from Ethan, to Brett, and settled on Nicole. A million questions hung between them.

"Oh, my." Mrs. Eggert's entire face transformed. Nicole

had anticipated anger, but instead she only saw something akin to gratitude. "Oh, he looks just like his father at that age. I don't know why I didn't see it before." Mrs. Eggert slid her arm over Ethan's shoulder and Ethan smiled up at his grandma. "Your daddy was such a handsome boy and so are you. I don't know why your mother—"

Mrs. Eggert shook her head. "That's a conversation for another day, I suppose."

Nicole clutched her hands together and watched the scene unfold in front of her. Suddenly, panic was pressing in from all sides. She felt trapped, twitchy. She wanted to run away.

Just as she had done eight years ago.

Dear Lord, help me do what's right for Ethan.

A quiet calm settled around her.

Brett held out his hand to his mother and Ethan. "Let's go outside where we can talk."

"Let's go to the house. Janice made breakfast." Mrs. Eggert adjusted the strap of her purse on her shoulder and turned toward the door with Ethan's hand in hers.

"Oh, I um…" Nicole met Brett's gaze, pleading with her eyes for him to slow this big family reunion down.

Brett leaned in close. "It would mean a lot to my mother if you and Ethan would come for breakfast." He turned his head to whisper closer to her ear and his cheek brushed against hers. "It's my father…"

Brett stepped away and locked eyes with her. "He's not doing well." Brett had shared this with her before. His gaze drifted behind her. He seemed lost in thought. "If you'd rather not go, I can bring Ethan home after brunch."

Dread washed over her. Already the Eggerts were trying to lure Ethan away. Her mind raced with the implications, even though she knew she was being paranoid. "No," her voice cracked, "I'd rather stay with Ethan. This is a lot for him to absorb. He needs this mother."

"Then come on." Brett gestured toward the exit.

Nicole was eager to catch up to Ethan and Mrs. Eggert. In the blink of an eye, Nicole felt like she was losing control.

A woman dressed in a gray uniform met Nicole, Brett and Ethan at the front door of the Eggerts's home. Mrs. Eggert had been driven home separately. On the way over, Nicole had called her grandmother to let her know their plans so she wouldn't worry.

When they stepped into the foyer, Nicole squeezed Ethan's hand and swallowed around a knot in her throat. She tried to keep her mouth shut as she took in the spiral staircase, fresh flowers on the table and the crystal chandelier. The home was even more impressive on the inside.

Brett smiled. "Hi, Janice."

The woman smiled brightly and tapped Brett on the arm with obvious affection. "You haven't come for Sunday brunch in a long time, Mr. Brett. Nice to see you."

"You, too." Brett placed his hand gently on the small of Nicole's back. "This is Nicole and her son, Ethan."

Janice smiled and Nicole thought she saw tears in the woman's eyes. "Ah, yes, I heard about Ethan." She held out her hand to greet them both. "So nice to meet you, Mr. Ethan."

Ethan took her hand and pumped it, a satisfied expression on his face.

"Is my mother in the dining room?" Brett asked.

"She will be soon. She went to get your father. She wanted to share the news before you arrived." Janice held out her arm. "Please, go into the dining room. Make yourself comfortable. Your parents will be in soon."

In the dining room, brunch was laid out on a wide side table. Nicole leaned over and whispered in Brett's ear. "Your mother goes all out."

Brett lifted an eyebrow, but didn't say anything.

"This is a pretty fancy house, isn't it?" Nicole nudged her son's shoulder. She hoped if she made idle happy chat, she could shake this horrible sense of dread she felt.

"Yeah. It's huge." Ethan plucked a fancy pastry from the side table and took a big bite. Crumbs sprinkled the floor.

"You're a guest. You need to wait." Nicole should have been horrified at her son's behavior, yet something deep inside was pleased. Pleased that her son wasn't daunted by his grandparents' wealth. As a kid, she had always been intimidated by those who lived in big fancy houses. It always made her feel *less than*. Perhaps her feelings of insecurity had been responsible for her poor choices. Her need to fit in…with a bad boy from a wealthy family.

She shook away the thought. She wasn't that girl anymore.

Brett laughed; the sound warmed Nicole's heart. "He's fine. Your grandmother likes to see her boys eat. It makes her feel good."

"You grew up in this house, Uncle Brett?" Ethan asked around a mouthful of pastry.

"Yes."

"My dad, too?" His eyes scanned the space.

"Your dad and I both grew up here." Brett lowered his voice. "When he was about your age, we got in trouble for playing ball in the house. We broke an expensive vase."

Ethan winced. "Bet your mom wasn't happy."

Brett shook his head, exaggerating the movement. "No. She. Wasn't."

Nicole studied Brett, thinking how he'd make a wonderful father. Then, feeling a little conspicuous, she said, "I can't believe you grew up in this house."

Brett wrinkled his nose. "You act like you've never been here."

Nicole laughed and cut a glance at her son, not wanting to say too much in front of him. "I haven't."

A muscle in Brett's jaw twitched. Shuffling outside the dining room drew their attention. Brett rushed into the foyer and took his father's elbow. "Here, Father."

His father pulled his arm away. "I'm fine. Don't treat me like an invalid." His father's shaky voice had hard-edged undertones.

"George, Ethan is here," Mrs. Eggert said, giving her husband a gentle reminder.

Nicole reached out and grabbed Ethan's hand and held it against her side. She prayed he wouldn't notice she was shaking. She knew her feelings were irrational, almost as if she were handing her child over for adoption. She struggled to draw in a decent breath. The elaborate display of brunch food and fresh flowers swirled into indistinguishable shades of browns, whites and yellows. The smell that had only moments ago made her stomach growl now made her nauseous.

She was crazy to come here. The Eggerts had said horrible things about her after Max died.

Mr. Eggert stepped into the room. His warm gray eyes landed on Ethan. He was a shell of the man he once was. Compassion stung the backs of her eyes.

Forgiveness.

Mr. Eggert extended his hand to Ethan. Nicole whispered, "It's okay, Ethan. This is your grandfather."

Ethan took a step forward. Mr. Eggert cupped his grandson's cheek and a shaky smile curved the older gentleman's lips. "You resemble your father."

Eight years of secrets weighed on Nicole's chest and made it hard to breathe. "I see it in his eyes." She met Brett's gaze. "I see the resemblance in both your sons' eyes."

Brett's mother stood with her hands clasped in front of

her. She seemed to be struggling to stay composed. "Are you hungry?" Her question was directed at her grandson.

Ethan nodded.

"What do you like to eat? We have just about anything you could like. Your father always liked peanut doughnuts."

Ethan's tentative smile grew wide. "I love peanut doughnuts, too."

Brett's mother led Ethan by the shoulder to the table and pointed out the doughnuts. "Have whatever you'd like." She smiled politely at Nicole. "As long as it's okay with your mother."

Nicole nodded. "Just don't make yourself sick."

"I won't." Ethan grabbed a white plate and loaded it up with a peanut doughnut, bacon and strawberries. The kid was in heaven.

Once everyone was seated at the table, they made idle conversation. Mrs. Eggert was charming, polite and friendly, so different from the woman Nicole had known. Could Nicole blame the woman for erecting a wall after the tremendous hurt and loss she had suffered after Max died?

A burden had been lifted from Nicole's shoulders. Her son had a family who loved him. How could that be bad?

When brunch was over, Mr. Eggert pushed back his chair and smiled at Ethan. "You have a great appetite, young man."

Ethan smiled in response, perhaps not knowing what to say.

"Would you like to see your father's room? Max loved baseball."

"George!" Mrs. Eggert admonished him. "Maybe you shouldn't rush things."

Mr. Eggert stood, seemingly with renewed energy. "It's okay. It would be good if the boy understood where he came from."

Nicole flicked a panicked look in Brett's direction. He tipped his head as if to say, "Everything's okay." She had to have faith.

Surely Mr. Eggert wouldn't whisk Ethan away and start bad-mouthing her, would he? Doubt twisted her up in knots. She'd never fully escape the insecure girl with low self-esteem and a drug habit.

Brett's father met Nicole's gaze. "We never redid Max's room. He had trophies from his baseball days and school yearbooks. That sort of thing. You're welcome to come along."

Immediately Nicole felt ashamed for thinking the worst. She closed her eyes briefly and took a deep breath. She thought a single word on her exhale.

Trust.

"That would be fine, Mr. Eggert." Nicole placed her fork on her empty plate and forced a smile.

Trust.

Brett placed his warm hand over hers and smiled. He mouthed, "It's okay."

Nicole nodded, but for some reason, despite her budding hope for a bright future, a terrible sense of foreboding swept in and darkened her mood.

The melodic chime of the Eggerts' doorbell interrupted the quiet cup of coffee Brett and Nicole were sharing in his parents' formal dining room.

Brett pushed back from the table. "I better get that. Janice is busy in the kitchen."

As Brett strode across the foyer, pounding shook the door. "What in the world?" he muttered. He held up his hand as Janice strode into the foyer. She stopped short, her eyes wide with concern. He reached the door and swung it open. A heavy feeling weighed in his gut that had nothing to do with the huge breakfast he had eaten.

Ed Hanson touched his hat. "Sir, I have an arrest warrant for Nicole Braun."

Brett's heart sank. Had their voices carried to the dining room? Brett stepped onto the porch and pulled the door closed. "What is this about?"

"This morning Derreck Denner called the police station. He said jewelry belonging to the deceased was found in Nicole's possession." He cleared his throat. "Do you know anything about this, sir?"

The closed door stood between them and Nicole. "Don't do this." Brett studied the piece of paper Ed handed him. Brett's pulse pounded in his ears. Ed had a warrant for Nicole's arrest. "How did you know Nicole was here?"

"I saw you leaving church with her, sir."

"I don't understand how you got the warrant for her arrest on a Sunday morning."

"I'm sorry, sir. You know how things can go in a small town. The Peters family knows the judge. The judge provided the arrest warrant."

Anger heated Brett's face. "Why didn't you call me?" He needed more time to prove Nicole had nothing to do with this. Someone was setting her up.

"Derreck called the judge directly. He suggested you were too close to Nicole to effectively do your job. Apparently, the jewelry was stolen during the time Nicole worked at the funeral home and it was found in her possession."

"You aren't going to arrest Nicole." Brett spoke the words through gritted teeth.

Ed raised a skeptical eyebrow. "Are you saying you're ignoring the warrant?"

"I'm your boss and you are *not* going to arrest her in front of her son."

Ed shifted his stance, clearly uncomfortable. "Don't make this harder than it has to be. I have a job to do."

Brett plowed his hand through his hair and shook his head. How many times had he used that line on people? *I'm only doing my job.*

The door creaked open. Nicole peered out, her eyes wide with worry. "What's going on?"

Ed unhooked his handcuffs from his belt and reached for Nicole's wrists. "I'm afraid you're under arrest, ma'am."

"Brett?" The single word escaped Nicole's quivering lips. All the color drained from her face.

"I'm sorry. They believe you stole the jewelry."

"Why? What?" Confusion and anger swept across her features. "Was this your plan? For me to bring Ethan here so I could be arrested?"

"No." Brett lowered his head and rubbed the back of his neck.

Nicole dropped her gaze to her shackled wrists. "I don't believe you."

Fast footsteps sounded on the ceramic tile. Ethan appeared in the doorway holding one of Max's baseball trophies. The smile slid from Ethan's face when his gaze landed on the handcuffs on his mom's wrists. "Mom?"

Nicole reached out awkwardly with her cuffed hands to comfort her son. "It's okay." She repeated the words that Brett had said only moments ago.

"Please, Ms. Braun, we have to go." Ed nudged Nicole toward his police cruiser.

Nicole pleaded with her eyes, but there was nothing Brett could do to spare her from this humiliation. "Please bring Ethan home to my grandmother's."

Brett nodded.

Nicole hiked her chin and set her jaw. Ed closed the cruiser door and Nicole stared straight ahead. Ethan wrapped his arms around Brett's waist and squeezed.

Brett patted the young boy's back. "Everything is going to be okay."

He was a big fat liar.

TWELVE

Nicole's teeth chattered incessantly. She wrapped her hands around the edge of the cool metal bench in the holding cell at the Silver Lake police headquarters. Tears burned the backs of her eyes, but she refused to cry. She would not show weakness in this place.

She tilted her head back and rested it against the hard cinder-block wall. When she had rolled out of bed this morning her only plan was church. Church, groceries and an afternoon with Ethan and Gigi.

Oh, Gigi.

Her grandmother would be crushed. And Ethan. He must be terrified.

A traitorous tear trailed down her cheek. Her throat constricted with a combination of panic, fear and betrayal.

How had she ended up here? Had Richard White been so determined to mess with her life that he planted the jewelry? She bowed her head and covered her face with her hands. As panic threatened, she quieted her mind by reciting the Lord's Prayer. She had to be strong for Ethan. She had to find a way out of this mess for him.

Everything she did was for Ethan.

Ed Hanson hadn't told her much when he brought her in. He claimed Brett wanted to talk to her himself. A new wave of fear swept over her. She felt as if she was eighteen again. An insecure eighteen-year-old who was newly pregnant and being blamed for her boyfriend's death.

Nicole bowed her head. *Dear Lord, please help me get*

through this. Please protect me and protect my son in my absence. Let Brett see the truth.

Distinct footsteps sounded on the concrete. She snapped her head up and squinted toward the sound. She blinked back the tears blurring her vision. She had to be tough. She sucked in a breath when Brett appeared, still wearing his church clothes.

He stood on the other side of the bars, one hand clasping the other wrist. "How are you?"

Nicole rose to her feet. "How am I?" She kept her voice low, but more than a hint of hysteria was evident. Brett was the chief of police. He could have stopped all this before it began. But he didn't. Had he been lying when he told her he believed in her innocence?

She swallowed her anger.

Trust.

"Did you take Ethan home?"

Brett bowed his head briefly then met Nicole's gaze with those warm brown eyes. "Ethan's with my mom and dad."

Nicole opened her mouth to protest and Brett cut her off. "He's with his grandparents."

She wrapped her hands around the bars and leaned as close to Brett as she could. "I don't want your mom to take care of my son. You need to get my son and drive him *home*. Tell Gigi I'll be home soon."

"Ethan is fine. He's helping my father sand the boat."

Her head pulsed with growing anger. "Why am I here? You don't believe I stole that jewelry, do you?"

Brett held up his finger. He pulled out a ring of keys and unlocked the jail cell. He offered her his hand, but she didn't take it. She brushed past him and swung around to confront him. "Why am I here? Why now?"

"I told Derreck that I found stolen jewelry in your shed.

He used that to get a warrant from the judge for your arrest."

Nicole stared at him, doubting everything she had come to feel about Brett. "Why would you tell him that? Did you want him to think I was a thief?" With Max she knew where she stood. He came around when he wanted something. She was a good time. The party girl. With Brett, she'd thought she rated higher.

She was still low on the food chain.

A girl from the wrong side of the tracks.

"I didn't steal the jewelry." She locked eyes with him. "I'm not going to plead with you to believe me. I'm telling the truth."

Brett touched her arm.

She jerked it away. "What happens now?"

"I promised your grandmother I'd bring you home."

"You told my grandmother, yet you left Ethan with your parents?" Nicole sighed.

"I didn't want her to worry when it got late."

She blinked a few times and a realization seeped in. "I can leave?"

"Yes. Your bail has been paid."

Hope and anger blossomed in her chest. She didn't want him to sweep in and save the day. She could stand on her own two feet, but today wasn't the time to be proud.

"How?"

"My mother."

Nicole sucked in a breath. "Your mother? Your mother paid my bail?" She jammed her fists into her hips.

"My mother doesn't want to see her grandson suffer."

Nicole swallowed. "You're the chief of police. You could have prevented my arrest."

A muscle ticked in Brett's jaw. "I was as surprised as you were."

She shook her head in disbelief. "Now I have to explain to my son why I was arrested."

"Tell him the truth."

"I'm done letting you or anyone else make me feel like I did something wrong when I didn't."

Brett cleared his throat. "Only you can make you feel like you did something wrong. Don't put so much weight into what other people say." He studied her face. Heat crawled up her neck and cheeks.

Brett put a hand on the small of her back. "Guess it's time to get you out of here. I'll drive you home."

"No, thanks." Nicole spun on her heel and quickened her pace toward the door.

Brett caught up to her and let his hand graze her lower back. She couldn't deny the feeling of security his proximity invoked. "I am going to drive you to my parents to pick up Ethan, then I'll take you home. If you don't want to accept my help as a friend, I'll insist on it as the chief of police."

"Okay, Officer." Nicole tried to sound flippant but in reality, she was relieved. Her reckless self would have done something stupid, like walk home alone. And considering someone had it in for her, she might be considered too stupid to live.

Brett walked Nicole and Ethan to the front door of Gigi's home. Ethan had been silent the entire drive home. Nicole stopped and muttered thanks for the ride. Her manners wouldn't allow her to not at least acknowledge that much. But in her foul mood, she still wanted to punish him. Punish him for not stopping the arrest. He *was* the chief of police.

Nicole kissed Ethan's head. She opened the front door and ushered him inside. "Go in and let Gigi know we're home. I'll be in in a minute."

Brett caught the storm door before it slammed. "Nicole…"

She held up her hand. "I'm really tired." She propped the storm door open with her shoulder.

Brett brushed his thumb across her cheek and she resisted the urge not to tilt her head into his hand. "Thanks for the ride."

"I'm going to help you through this."

"How?" Her throat felt parched. "By making sure I have a nice dry cell for the next ten years?" She was going for sarcasm, but fear and frustration won out.

He stared at her a long minute. Too long. She could see the doubt in his eyes, mirroring the fear in her heart. "I'll do everything I can to get to the bottom of this. But sometimes these things take time to play out."

Nicole's heart dropped. "Meanwhile lives are ruined." She turned to go inside. "Thanks for everything." This time there was no mistaking her sarcasm.

Nicole slipped off her coat and tossed it over the back of the chair in her grandmother's kitchen. The TV room was dark, save for the familiar flickering of the screen. She crept in. Gigi wasn't in her usual spot. Her wheelchair was next to the couch. Ethan was lying across the couch and her grandmother was smoothing Ethan's hair off his forehead. Gigi smiled at Nicole, a sad smile that broke her heart.

Nostalgia twisted her insides. Nicole herself had fallen asleep on Gigi's lap many times when she was a child. Gigi had been her only constant in a volatile world. An ache started in the back of her throat. Gigi eventually wouldn't be around for Ethan if anything happened to her.

Ethan stared blankly at the TV and Nicole quickly swiped at a tear trailing down her cheek. She crossed the brown sculptured carpet and knelt down in front of him.

"I'm glad you're home." Gigi was the first to speak.

"Brett drove us home." She locked gazes with her grandmother, whose stern look said more than any words, mimicking her own concerns. *Can you trust him?*

Ethan scrunched up his nose and scratched it with the back of his hand.

"Let's get you to bed." Nicole doubted she'd be able to lift him if he fell asleep on the couch.

Ethan adjusted his gaze to land squarely on her. It reminded Nicole of how he used to watch her—study her—when she held him in her arms as a baby. "Why were you in jail?" He finally asked the question heavy on his heart.

Nicole tucked a sweaty strand of hair behind his ear. "The police made a mistake. I would never do anything that was against the law."

"I know," Ethan said in the matter-of-fact way kids often did when they perceived things to be black and white. "Were you scared?"

"A little." Ethan scooted around to a seated position and grabbed her hand. He absentmindedly traced her thumbnail, something he had done since he was a toddler. "But Uncle Brett told me everything was going to be all right. And my new grandparents were really nice, too."

"That's good." Nicole swallowed hard. It pained her to know she wasn't there for her son when he needed her most.

"You're blessed to have lots of family," Gigi added for reassurance.

Ethan scooted toward the edge of the couch. "How come you never told me my dad liked to play T-ball?"

I didn't know. I didn't know a lot about your father.

"When can I go over there again? They're going to tell me more stories about my dad when he was a kid."

"We'll make plans." Nicole bit her bottom lip. "But right now, I think you better get to bed."

Ethan stood and hugged Nicole around her waist, very

tightly. She ran her hand down his head. "I missed you, Mom. Don't ever, ever, ever go away again."

Nicole swallowed back a promise that was out of her control. "I love you so much."

"I love you, too, Mom."

Nicole helped Ethan into his pajamas and tucked him under his superhero comforter. She had never been more grateful for the little things in life. To kiss her only child good-night.

She backed out of the room. She blew him a kiss, then pulled the door closed.

What if she couldn't prove her innocence? What if she went to jail for a long time?

Brett answered his phone and pressed it to his ear. *Nicole.* "I'm surprised you called." He unlocked the door to his house and stepped inside.

He heard Nicole sigh heavily over the line. "I apologize for being rude to you when you dropped me off."

"I'll give you a pass. All things considered."

Her incredulous snort made him smile. He tossed his keys on the kitchen table and surveyed his empty home, sparsely decorated. A true bachelor pad, his mother called it.

"I feel I need to clear the air.... My past doesn't give you a lot of reason to trust me."

He rubbed his palm against his cheek, but didn't say anything. He sat down on his overstuffed brown couch and leaned back, closing his eyes. He could imagine Nicole's worried eyes as she paced circles.

"I want to trust you." He sank deeper into the couch. Time for full honesty. "But I got burned once."

"By a girl?" Brett thought he detected a wistfulness in her tone.

"No. I got burned by Max."

Silence stretched across the line.

Brett leaned forward, resting his elbows on his thighs and closing his eyes. "I knew Max was involved in a lot of bad stuff, but he told me he was done. He told me he was clean." An image of his brother's smiling face flashed in his mind's eye. "And I believed him."

Brett heard Nicole sniff and he wondered if she was crying.

Brett sighed heavily. "My life changed forever the day he wrapped his car around the tree. I should have known he was lying. I should have never let him out of my sight."

"You were his brother. Not his father." Her voice was soft, comforting. "Don't do that to yourself."

"You mean, blame myself?" he scoffed.

"Exactly. It took me a long time to forgive myself. It was hard to do because so many other people hadn't forgiven me. Still haven't." Her voice grew quiet. "I think your mom is coming around."

"You made her very happy. I haven't seen both my parents this happy in a long time."

"Good." Brett couldn't glean much from her single word. Was she happy, too, or did she regret allowing Ethan to know his grandparents?

"I was the one who convinced my parents Max was clean. They gave him back his car the morning he died."

"Oh…" Shocked emotion rippled down the phone line. "I didn't know." She cleared her throat. "In the end, Max made his own choices. For years I lay awake at night wishing I could have stopped him from driving away from me."

"Max wouldn't have had the car if I hadn't gone to our parents and vouched for him."

"Max could be persuasive."

Brett laughed, the sound empty and hollow. "You're telling me."

"You have to stop beating yourself up over this. You

did what you thought was right. Only Max is to blame for all the mistakes he made." Nicole sniffed. "But of all the mistakes I've made, I'll never regret one thing."

"Ethan."

"Yes. Ethan." He heard her sigh. "I was young and irresponsible, but in the end, my son is one of my greatest blessings."

"I'm sorry my family and I hurt you." Brett wished she was sitting next to him so he could pull her hand into his and hold it.

"I have no choice but to stick around and prove my innocence. I have Ethan to consider now."

THIRTEEN

"I can't believe it." Nicole tilted her head and leaned back against the passenger seat. Brett stared through the salt-spattered windshield at the No Parking Here to Corner sign on the narrow Buffalo street, pondering their next move. Meeting with Abe King's son had been a total bust.

Nicole shifted in her seat and touched his hand with ice-cold fingers. "Do you really think this was a good idea, to come to Buffalo to talk to the King family? What if they call the funeral home? Mr. Peters and Derreck won't be happy we're interfering."

"We had to try." Brett ran his hand along the top of the steering wheel. "There seems to be two suspicious things going on at the funeral home. Jewelry has gone missing and a client has accused the funeral home of ripping them off."

Nicole sighed heavily. "Isaac King seemed satisfied the matter has been resolved."

"What if Mr. Peters just settled up with the King family so they wouldn't keep pushing the issue?"

Nicole worked her bottom lip. "Why would Mr. Peters refund the difference between the original contract and the new one, if the funeral home had a valid new contract? The difference in contracts was a few thousand dollars. Not exactly chump change."

Brett covered her hand and squeezed. "Mr. Peters is a businessman. He probably figured the bad press from this—coupled with the jewelry thefts—" he thought he detected a deeper pink color in Nicole's cheeks "—could ruin his business. The King family said Mr. Peters didn't want them to suffer any more in their time of grief."

Nicole pulled her hand away and tucked it under her thigh. "I can't help but wonder if Derreck has anything to do with this?"

Brett studied her face. "His aunt speaks fondly of him."

Nicole sighed heavily. "I don't know what to think. Derreck has rubbed me the wrong way from the beginning. He's a bit condescending, like funeral work is beneath him." Nicole looked down briefly.

"I heard he wasn't really keen on the funeral home initially. I'm sure he came back because he figured it would be more lucrative than signing up customers for two-year cell phone plans."

"Yeah, working at a cell phone provider must have been tedious work." Nicole tapped her fingers on the door armrest. "All I know is that someone is trying to ruin my life. The one person who does hate me would have a tough time accessing the jewelry—" she hitched her shoulders, then let them drop "—unless Richard White found a way to rob the graves." She ran a hand across her chin. "But that seems over the top even for a creep like Richard. And if it's not Derreck trying to shift the focus from something underhanded he's doing..." She stared out the windshield, lost in thought.

"What about Mr. Peters?"

"Mr. Peters?" She met his gaze with a thoughtful expression. "Doubtful. I mean...why?"

Brett stared at her intently. "What better way to get away with something than to set someone else up? He's the one who hired you, right? Despite your rumored background." Adrenaline spiked his pulse. "Maybe he wanted to have you working there so he could shift the blame if someone uncovered the embezzlement."

Nicole lifted a shaky hand to her mouth, then dropped

it. "No, not Mr. Peters. He's too kind. And why steal from his own funeral home? You've seen their house. He doesn't need the money."

Brett lifted an eyebrow. "Looks can be deceiving."

Nicole yanked on her seat belt as if she were working all the details over in her mind. "This entire mess started the same day I was supposed to meet with the King family. If the weather and my grandmother's health hadn't stopped me…" She shook her head and closed her eyes briefly. "If Mr. King really made changes to his prearrangement at the funeral home, why didn't he tell his family?"

"Maybe he died before he had a chance."

Nicole scratched her head. "What is going on? Why is someone trying to make it look like I'm stealing jewelry?"

Brett ran his hand along the steering wheel. "Let's take possible embezzlement off the table. *Who* would want to make it look like you're stealing from the funeral home?"

"Richard White." She rubbed the back of her neck.

"I talked to Richard more than once. He claims he wants to put the past behind him. To date, we have nothing to connect him to the stolen jewelry." Brett drummed his fingers on the steering wheel. "Richard gets angrier each time I show up on his doorstep. You are definitely not his favorite person."

"That goes both ways," Nicole muttered.

Brett smacked the steering wheel. "Let's hit a few pawnshops. If someone had a chance to steal jewelry, why just steal a few select pieces? Maybe he stole more than what he planted in your possession. Maybe he pawned the rest. Do you think you would recognize stolen pieces?"

Nicole's silence wasn't exactly a ringing endorsement of his idea. Finally she said, "Yes, I think so, but it's probably a waste of time."

Doubt crept in. Why didn't Nicole want him scouring

pawnshops? He shook away the thought. He had to learn to trust. She wasn't his brother.

"Won't that be like searching for a needle in a haystack?" Her voice sounded weary. It had been a long few days.

"You underestimate my investigative skills."

"Nowadays people can sell things on the internet. Ever hear of Craigslist?"

He narrowed his gaze. "Are you talking from experience?"

"Yes."

Brett's heart sank.

"Take it easy, Inspector Clouseau. As a single mother with limited funds, I tend to scour Craigslist and eBay for deals. Not everyone can afford to walk into a store and pay full price for things." Her irate glare pierced his heart.

"Since we're in Buffalo, let's visit a few pawnshops first, then we can check online. The owners will have to show me the paperwork. It's illegal to sell stolen goods." His lips thinned. "I'll need you to identify the jewelry. Are you okay with that?"

"Yes, I'm not going to let someone ruin my life. I want to figure out who's doing this to me."

"Okay." Brett shoved the gear into Drive. "But you're going to only say and do what I tell you."

"Yes, sir." She snapped her seat belt into place. "Let's roll."

Nicole wrapped her hand around the door handle of the You Need Cash We Pawn pawnshop. Brett whispered in her ear, "Remember, just like in the last shop."

"And the one before that." Nicole tipped her head from side to side to ease the tension knotting her neck. "We're wasting our time." She was eager to go home, pull Ethan into her arms, put on a kid movie and forget about the world crumbling around her. Hard to imagine she used to think her life was boring. She'd do anything to have a boring life again with a nine-to-five job. Her grandmother's social security check was getting stretched pretty thin.

"Remember," Brett continued his instructions, "pretend you're shopping. Scan the jewelry. If you see a familiar piece, ask to see it. Once you know it's a piece from the funeral home—"

"I know, I know. Pretend I want to buy it. Then the clerk will have to pull the paperwork."

A smile brightened his handsome face. "We make pretty good partners."

Nicole rolled her eyes. She turned and pushed the door open before she said or did something stupid. "Let's get this over with."

Nicole's heart raced as she scanned the displays. Sports cards, antique toys, watches, jewelry. She had reached the end of the counter when an ornate rosary with a gold cross caught her attention. She remembered it because Mrs. O'Connor's daughter had told her that her mother received the rosary as a gift from her friend who had traveled to the Vatican. Her mother had taken great comfort during the final stages of her illness knowing she possessed a rosary that had been blessed by the Pope.

Nicole cleared her throat. "I'd like to see the rosary."

The young man behind the counter took his time finishing his text before he put his cell phone down and found the key to open the display case. "What did you want to see?"

"Um, the rosary."

The young man scanned the row of necklaces, rings and watches. Nicole was about to explode. "I'd like to see the white beads next to the gold watch."

Finally, the clerk, Brad, according to his yellow name tag, grabbed the rosary and plunked it down on the counter. The delicate blue lace design on the beads that separated groups of ten beads cemented it for Nicole. With shaky hands, she picked it up and turned to Brett. "I'd like this."

He put his warm hand under hers. "This rosary?"

"Yes." Her pulse thrummed in her ears. "This rosary."

Brett pulled his wallet out and flashed his badge. "I'd like to see the paperwork for this item."

Without a word, Brad shuffled to the file cabinet in the corner. He pulled out a slip of paper and handed it to Brett. "They want to sell it. A hundred bucks."

Nicole's eyes were drawn to the bottom of the slip. She jerked her head back and fuzziness clouded her brain. She squinted again at the signature line of the transaction slip.

Her signature.

The next day, in the cramped kitchen, Gigi stared up at Nicole from her wheelchair. "You haven't said much since—"

"My arrest?" Nicole plopped into the kitchen chair.

"Yes." Her grandmother wiped her fingers on her napkin. "Ethan's at school. We can talk. Really talk."

Nicole wrapped her arms tightly around her middle. She felt numb. She was fortunate Brett didn't arrest her again after the pawnshop fiasco. Thankfully, he seemed to believe her when she said her signature had been forged.

"I'm sorry, Gigi, I really don't want to talk about it. Not unless Brett comes in here and tells me they have the person who's determined to mess up my life."

Gigi covered Nicole's hand with her own. "Your mother never wanted to talk, either. She'd storm in here and complain about her life and storm back out. She kept everyone away. I could never reach her."

Nicole stiffened. She had worked her entire life to not be like her mother. And here she was, a single mother, unemployed, and with an arrest record. She plunked her chin down on the heel of her hand and stared at the marks in the old kitchen table.

Her grandmother squeezed her hand. The expression on Gigi's face softened her heart. "You, my dear, are not your mother. Your mother was unable to stop the vicious downward cycle. You got your life back on track once you found out you were pregnant. You put Ethan before everything else. You're just experiencing a little setback."

Nicole choked and laughed at the same time. "A little setback, huh? I love your outlook."

"What about your faith? This is the time you need to rely on it. Now, more than ever."

Nicole slumped into the hard chair and jammed her hands into the pockets of the jacket she was still wearing. Her fingers brushed against her mittens. She pulled them out and smoothed them on the table.

A sad smile pulled at the corners of her grandmother's mouth. "I taught your mom how to knit." Gigi picked up one of the mittens and traced the pattern with her index finger. "I remember sitting on the couch next to her, our knitting needles clacking, chatting about her day at school."

Nostalgia tightened her throat. Finally she found her words. "How old was my mother when you taught her to knit?" The image her grandmother had painted was unlike any she associated with her mother.

"Eleven." Her grandmother's eyes grew misty. "I started to lose her when she hit her teenage years." She studied the backs of her hands. "I couldn't get her back."

"I'm afraid I'm going to lose Ethan."

Her grandmother slipped her hand inside the mitten. "You won't lose Ethan. I know you're not responsible for the thefts at the funeral home. Chief Eggert will get to the bottom of this."

Nicole bowed her head. "The pawnshop had my signature and a copy of my driver's license."

Doubt flashed in her grandmother's eyes, or maybe Nicole had imagined it. Heat swept up her neck and face.

"Did you lose your license?"

Nicole shook her head. "I checked. It's still in my purse."

"Who could have had access to your purse? To your license?"

"I suppose anyone I worked with. I kept my purse in a cabinet at the funeral home. Someone could have slipped out the license, copied and returned it." She sighed heavily. A throbbing persisted behind her eyes. "Brett's investigating all the angles. I mean, why would I point out the rosary at the pawnshop if I were the one who had stolen it?"

Her grandmother reached out and grabbed her hand. "I have faith in you. You must learn to have faith in yourself." She paused a moment. "And others. It's okay to accept help." She patted the tops of her legs. "I've had to learn to accept help, too."

Nicole stood and kissed the top of her grandmother's head. "I'm happy to be here for you." She just wasn't happy about the circumstances. She walked away, braced herself on the edge of the kitchen sink and stared over the backyard.

No job. No job prospects. *Who's going to hire someone who's been accused of stealing from their employer?*

The weight of the world pressed heavily on her shoulders.

She'd get through this. She had to.

Her cell phone chirped on the table. The caller ID indicated it was Ethan's school. Her heart sank. *Please don't be misbehaving, buddy. I can't deal with that right now.*

She drew in a deep breath. "Hello."

"Is this Ms. Braun?"

"Yes." Her heart beat loudly in her ears.

"This is the main office at Ethan's school. I'm afraid Ethan has been very disruptive in gym class. He kicked another child." The woman's deep voice had a nasal quality, reminding Nicole of the old switchboard operators portrayed on TV. "I sent Ethan to the principal's office. I believe she's going to suspend him for a few days, but I'm sure if you came down, we could work something out. The gym teacher is sympathetic to your situation, but she just couldn't have him disrupting class again."

"I appreciate your calling. I'll come down right now."

"Oh, that would be great. Ethan is a good boy. He just needs a little guidance." The woman's tone—once Nicole got past the nasal part—was a mix of compassion and condescension.

Nicole tried not to bristle at the comment. "Thank you."

She ended the call and found her grandmother staring up at her. "Ethan. He was acting up in gym."

Her grandmother smiled. "That kid has spunk."

"That kid better tone down his spunk or he's going to get kicked out of school." She grabbed her coat and at the same time dialed Brett's number.

Her grandmother waved her hand. "He's only seven."

"He needs a strong male role model in his life."

Her grandmother tipped her head. "You can't find a stronger role model than the chief of police."

Nicole pressed her fingers to her temple, wondering what kind of future she and Brett had considering everything that was going on. She tugged on her knit cap. "I better get up to school to talk to the principal."

Brett's curt greeting came across the line and she pressed the phone to her ear. "Um, are you busy?"

"Yeah, I'm on a call. Did you need something?" His question came out more like, "I really don't have time even if you did need something."

"No, no, it can wait. I'll let you go."

"Okay." Brett ended the call.

Nicole realized Brett had a job to do, but the abrupt disconnect made her wonder if he was reconsidering her innocence. She sweated under her knit cap.

"I'm going to have to hoof it to the elementary school. I have my cell phone if you need anything."

"Okay, dear. Make sure you dress warmly."

Nicole clapped with her mittens. "I'm good. Maybe the walk in the cold will clear my head."

FOURTEEN

Nicole tugged on the ends of her scarf, tightening it around her neck. Wow, it was colder out here than she had anticipated. She quickened her pace. Once she got moving she'd warm up. Or so she convinced herself. The snow crunched under her boots. She needed to get to school so the principal understood she was a good parent and Ethan was just going through a rough patch.

Anxiety spurred her on. She was angry with herself for not following up more closely with the insurance company regarding her car. She had to get a replacement, sooner rather than later. Walking was a great form of exercise, but not in the dead of winter.

Out of the corner of her eye, she noticed a long car pulling up alongside the curb. She turned and was surprised to see an ancient pale-green hearse. The tinted passenger window cranked down.

"Nicole," Gene called, leaning across the passenger seat. "Need a ride?"

An inexplicable uneasiness wound its way up her spine. She wasn't exactly a child and Gene wasn't exactly a stranger. But accepting a ride in a hearse didn't sound like fun. "I don't want to inconvenience you." She kept walking.

The hearse crept forward.

"No inconvenience. And don't worry. I don't have a body in here." Gene pushed open the passenger door. "Come on. You'll freeze to death out there."

Nicole hesitated. "I have a meeting at the elementary school."

"Come on then. You don't want to be late."

"You might scare the kids."

"Are you kidding? They love the hearse. They wave at me all the time."

Nicole fisted her hands inside her mittens. She imagined Ethan, scared and alone, waiting outside the principal's office. She felt her resistance waning.

"Okay." She climbed over a mound of snow, stepping into the street then into the hearse. She slammed the door and it groaned loudly on its hinges. The interior smelled stale, like old socks. She couldn't imagine why. She ran her hand under her nose. "Thanks, Gene." The eight track tape in the dash caught her attention. "Is this your personal vehicle?"

Gene laughed. "Like it? Mrs. Peters had it stored in the funeral home garage for years. She gave it to me. She's always been nice to me like that."

Nicole shifted in her seat and a ripped piece of vinyl scraped across the back of her thigh. Out of the corner of her eye, she noticed a cheap pine casket in the back. "I thought you didn't have a body." She wrapped her fingers around the door release.

"I don't. I would never use this hearse to pick up a body." Gene dragged his long fingers through his combover. "I had to pick up a casket." His eyebrows disappeared under his bangs. "Cheap one. Some people are cheap until the end."

Nicole shrugged but didn't say anything. Some people who chose cremation also chose an inexpensive casket. Made no sense to burn an expensive one.

Gene put the gear into Drive and slanted her a sideways glance. "Good thing I came along when I did."

She nodded but didn't say anything. She'd have to be in

this car for five minutes tops, but right now making small talk with Gene Gentry seemed insurmountable. He wasn't exactly the most social guy. That's why his stopping to offer her a ride seemed out of the ordinary.

Nicole slumped back into the seat and sighed. She loosened the top two buttons on her thick winter coat. At the turn for the school, Gene went straight. Nicole shot upright. She pointed down Elm Street. "The elementary school is that way."

"I know." Gene gripped the steering wheel tighter with long thin fingers and white knuckles.

Nicole's stomach lurched. "You can let me out here. I'll walk." She reached for the door handle and Gene pressed his foot to the floor. The engine on the old hearse revved, seemingly up to the challenge.

"What are you doing?" Panic sent goose bumps coursing over her skin and her voice grew high-pitched.

"Hello, is this Ethan's mom?" Gene cut her a glance, an evil gleam in his eye. All the air rushed out of her lungs. "Your son has been acting up in gym class. He kicked another boy. Blah, blah, blah."

The deep, nasal voice from the school office.

"Pretty good, huh?" Gene smacked the steering wheel with his hand. "I fooled you, huh? Did you really think I was a woman?" He sounded almost giddy.

"Why?" Terror flooded hot and cold through her veins. "Why are you doing this to me?"

Gene tightened his long fingers around the steering wheel and stared blankly ahead.

Brett felt badly about being so abrupt with Nicole when she called, but he had been out on a call. Turns out someone—probably a bored teenager—smashed a rock through a warehouse window. Since the warehouse had an alarm, he'd had to go check it out. Lucky him. A brick. An alarm. And tons of paperwork.

When he was finishing up with the paperwork, his cell phone rang. A smile curved his lips when he recognized Nicole's home number.

"Hey there." He tossed the paperwork on the seat next to him, relieved to be able to apologize to Nicole for being abrupt earlier.

"Chief Eggert?" An elderly woman's voice came across the line.

He straightened in his seat. "Gigi? Is something wrong?"

"I'm not sure," she spoke quietly. "Nicole left a while ago to meet with Ethan's principal, but the school called moments ago to say that Ethan was acting up in the library and needed to speak with his mother. "I called Nicole's cell phone. She's not answering."

"I don't understand."

"Neither do I. Nicole should have already been at the school. However, she's not there and the school doesn't know anything about an incident in the gym."

Brett jammed his key in the ignition. "Where's Ethan?"

"He's at school waiting outside the principal's office." Panic edged Gigi's soft voice.

"Hang tight. I'll go to the school and get Ethan." He paused a moment. "I'm sure Nicole's okay."

"Thank you." Brett heard rustling and imagined Gigi stretching to hang up the phone on the wall.

Brett's pulse ticked in his ears. He called Nicole's cell phone. No answer. Icy dread settled in his gut. It wasn't like Nicole to drop off the radar.

Brett cruised past Nicole's home and continued in the direction of the school. No sign of Nicole along the way. When he reached the school office, Ethan looked up, a mix of relief and confusion on his face.

"Hi, Uncle Brett." Ethan's forehead wrinkled. "Where's my mom?"

Brett glanced around, hoping someone would have an answer. "Got held up. So, I'm the pinch hitter."

"Like in baseball." Ethan's eyes lit up.

"Exactly." Brett held out his hand for Ethan. "Now where's this principal?"

A woman in her early fifties stuck her head out the door. "Right here. Please, come in."

Ethan squeezed his uncle's hand and something in Brett's heart shifted. The principal explained that Ethan had been roughhousing in the library and had knocked a display of books over.

Brett gave Ethan his best stern do-you-really-think-that-was-the-best-idea look.

"Perhaps Ethan would do well with some counseling. Teach him appropriate behavior."

"He's a seven-year-old boy."

The principal's eyes dropped to Ethan who was staring out the window. "He's rambunctious. I'm afraid we can't continue to deal with these disruptions."

"What if I promise I'll personally provide guidance for the child?"

The principal seemed to consider this a moment. "He could use that." She leaned closer and mouthed the words, "His mother seems to be struggling. I've heard, well…" She gave a pointed glare at Ethan.

Brett bit back a retort. Why was everyone so quick to judge?

Hadn't he done the same thing?

Brett stood. "I think Ethan and I are going to play hooky for the rest of the day. The school day's almost over, right?"

The principal's eyes widened. "I suppose. Let me call his grandmother first." She squinted at the computer screen. "She *is* his emergency contact. I can't release him without her or his mother's authorization."

Brett waited a minute while the principal talked to Gigi and got her okay.

"Have a good afternoon." Brett took Ethan's hand and led him out of the office.

Brett swung by Ethan's classroom to grab his coat. When they hit the brisk cold air outside, Ethan turned to Brett. "Wow! You can do anything when you're the chief of police. Even skip school."

Brett couldn't help but smile. "Not *anything*." He crouched in front of his nephew. "You have to promise me you'll behave in school, okay?"

Ethan dipped his chin and shoved some snow around with the toe of his boot. "Okay." He stuffed his hands into his jacket pockets. "I get bored sometimes."

"We all get bored. You have to find better ways to occupy yourself. Like in the library. You could have searched for a book on something you really like instead of horsing around with the other boys."

"Like famous baseball players?" Ethan's eyes brightened.

"Exactly." Brett patted him on the back. "No more calls from school."

Ethan nodded. "Where *is* my mom?"

Brett's stomach plummeted. He wished he knew.

"Let's get you home. Maybe she's there." But a nagging feeling told Brett she wasn't.

Gene pulled the hearse down a snow-covered road way out in the country. He had warned her that if she tried to jump out of the vehicle, he would stop the car, shoot her and leave her to die on the side of the road. Like an animal.

Nicole had never heard Gene string so many words together.

The stale air in the hearse made it difficult to fill her lungs. When had Gene turned so nasty? At the funeral home, he had been quiet, distant almost. Socially awkward, but never...

All the newscasts of neighbors saying the mass murderer was quiet and shy slammed into her brain.

She breathed in slowly through her nose and let it out between tight lips. "How did you know I'd walk to the school? I could have called Brett for a ride."

Gene never took his eyes off the road, but even from this angle, she could tell he was gloating. "I made sure he was out on a call." He curled his arm showing his strength. "I set an alarm off at an old warehouse by throwing a brick through the window."

Nicole focused on her breathing, fearing she'd hyperventilate.

Gene leaned forward, wrapped his long fingers around the steering wheel and squinted against the increasing flurry of snowflakes. "And I knew you'd be walking since...you know, since your car got a little..." he cut a gaze toward her "...wet."

Nicole's mouth grew dry. "You caused Missy's accident?"

Gene laughed. "You were supposed to be in the car. You're too nosy. I borrowed one of the deceased's cars. A little red one. His daughter had it stored in a garage with the keys tucked over the visor. I'm sure they never missed it or even noticed the little scrape."

Nicole ran her hand along the door's vinyl armrest while Gene gloated. Her mind raced with possible escape scenarios. One seemed less feasible than the next.

Be smart. You won't get a second chance.

The wipers skidded across the slushy windshield. Gene muttered something about needing new blades. As he messed with the speed of the wipers, Nicole pulled her cell phone from her pocket and held it low between her thigh and the door. She had several missed calls. Her pulse beat wildly in her ears. She pressed Brett's number and tucked the phone against her thigh. Gene was distracted, adjusting the wipers between fast and super-fast.

Nicole closed her eyes briefly and prayed Brett would pick up and listen.

"I used to come out here as a kid. Is this the peanut trail?" She tried to sound nonchalant, but she knew she failed miserably.

"Shut up," Gene hissed. "These stupid wipers."

"Did you ever ride your bike on the peanut trail?"

Gene narrowed his gaze and pulled over. "What do you have over there?" Before she could answer, he reached across her lap and snagged the cell phone. His lips twisted into a sardonic grin. Staring at her, he powered the cell phone down and threw it out the window into the woods.

"Don't get any more goofy ideas."

Nicole glared at him. "Why are you doing this?"

Gene slammed the car into Drive and drove for a bit more. At some spot that seemed predetermined, he backed the hearse between two large pine trees. Gene climbed out and Nicole decided this was her one and only chance.

She yanked open the door and climbed out. She lost her footing in the deep snow, but decided to make a run for it anyway. A shot zinged past her head. She froze, instinctively lifting her hands like a criminal surrounded by the police.

Slowly she turned. Gene leveled a gun at her head. His eyes seemed dead. "Where are you going?"

Nicole held her hands in front of her. "Don't do this. I have a son."

"Your son will be better off without you."

"I'm his mother."

Gene shook his head, disgust on his face. "You never

cared about anyone's feelings when you were in high school. You hung around with all the cool kids." He used air quotes with one hand, the gun still aimed at her head with the other. "You all made my life miserable."

Nicole racked her brain. She knew Max and his friends could be brutal, but she'd never gotten involved. Maybe that was part of the problem. She never got involved. She never helped anyone, either.

"I'm sorry. My teenage years were pretty bad, too. I didn't mean to hurt you."

Something flashed, then extinguished in his eyes. "It doesn't matter. I have a job to do."

"A job?" Alarm bells clamored in her head. What she knew deep down in her heart sprang to her lips. "Is someone trying to cover up embezzling at the funeral home?" When he didn't answer, she said, "Stealing is one thing, but murder? Gene, please…"

Gene's unfocused gaze grew clearer. "Always do your job. That's what my dad said. Do your job. Don't give them a reason to fire you."

"Who are you doing this job for?" Nicole's jaw trembled. Hysteria pushed in from all sides. If she lost it, she'd never be able to think clearly. "Who would want to hurt me?"

"Stop talking. You're hurting my head." Gene blinked a few times, as if trying to process her questions. He shook his head, snapping out of it. He opened the back gate of the hearse and pointed at it with his gun. "Get in."

Nicole angled her head. "Get in?"

"Climb into the casket."

Nicole shook her head slowly. Her vision tunneled. "You'll have to kill me first."

Gene leveled the gun at her heart. "Okay."

Nicole lifted her hands. "No, no, no. I'll get in."

A wicked smile stretched across his waxy lips. "I've

made this game a little fair. I drilled holes in the casket. Maybe your new boyfriend will find you before it's too late. But I doubt it."

Nicole's mind raced, but she didn't want to ask questions that might set Gene off.

"Get in!" he yelled.

"Please, I hung around a rough crowd in high school. I'm sorry if me or my friends hurt you. I never meant it."

He adjusted his grip on the gun.

"I have a son who needs me."

Gene ran his sleeve under his nose and the gun swept past his face. "Get in or I'll shoot you and shove you in myself."

Tiny stars danced in her line of vision. She pulled her mitten out of her pocket and discreetly dropped it under the rear bumper. She scooted into the back of the hearse, barely squeezing between the coffin and the side of the vehicle. Gene propped up the lid of the casket. "Climb in."

Reciting a prayer over and over in her head, Nicole slipped into the casket. Gene hovered over her like a creepy mourner at a wake peering into the casket of someone he was happy to be rid of. Up this close, his skin appeared almost translucent. "I'll be back." He lowered the lid.

Nicole slammed her fist against it. "No, don't do this."

An impatient expression swept across his face. "I really will be back. I need to shoot you. Make your death look like a suicide." He pressed the gun under her chin and his eyes narrowed. Nausea clogged her throat.

"Then why…" her parched mouth made it difficult to swallow "…then why are you burying me alive?"

A twinkle lit his sinister eyes. "I want to have some fun first. Make you suffer. Make you think about how you treated me in high school."

"Please…" Nicole begged. "I should have treated you

better. I didn't know." Her mind scrambled. "I won't sur-
vive. I'll suffocate. Even with the holes."

"That's a chance I'm willing to take."

Before she had a chance to say another word, Gene
slammed down the lid.

A moment later, Nicole felt jostling. Her stomach roiled.
*Breathe. Breathe. If I panic, I'll never get out of here.
Breathe. Breathe.*

She was being pulled. In the casket. Panic crowded in
on her, making her thoughts jumble. She had to get out
of here.

"Gene! Gene! Gene! Please, Gene!"

The casket tipped and she braced her hands against the
satin fabric. One end hit the ground, then the other end
came slamming down, jarring her teeth.

"Gene!" she screamed until her throat was raw. "Please,
let me out." He dragged the casket. She felt another jostle
and a thud. As if he had just dragged the box into a hole.
She breathed in slowly through her nose, trying to quell
the nausea. "Gene!" She stopped shouting and listened
to a dragging sound. Perhaps branches scraping across
the casket?

Panic squeezed all the air out of her lungs.

"Gene, let me out!"

Panic was winning. Making her dizzy. Time ticked on
and on until what seemed like an eternity passed. She sent
up a silent prayer. A prayer for calmness. A prayer for insight. A prayer she'd find a way out.

The sound of her breath—*in and out, in and out*—was
her only companion. Gene had left her buried in the middle of the woods.

In a coffin.

To die.

FIFTEEN

No one had seen Nicole in several hours. Brett drummed his fingers on the steering wheel of his cruiser. This was not good. Definitely not good.

And it seemed someone had called to lure her out of the house.

Brett retraced the route she would have taken to the school. No sign of her. He called the station and told dispatch to have the other officers keep an eye out for her. It wasn't protocol to have the police search for an adult so soon after her disappearance, but Brett knew Nicole wouldn't wander off. She had intended to meet with the principal and she'd never let Ethan down.

Where could she be?

Brett let out a long breath and tingling shot through his chest. He dialed dispatch again. "I'm headed over to the cemetery to talk to Richard White. Contact me immediately if anyone hears from Nicole."

Brett ended the call, checked for traffic and made a quick U-turn. He needed to have a little talk with the gravedigger. The ring of his cell phone startled him out of his thoughts. He snatched it up, praying for good news.

Praying. Just as he had done before he lost faith. Before he had lost Max.

Forgive me, Lord, for not trusting in you. Please let me find Nicole. Bring her home safely.

He answered the call. "Chief Eggert."

"Brett, it's Ed. I heard you're looking for Nicole. When did you last see her?"

"Nicole's grandmother said she left her house on foot on the way to the elementary school."

"What time?"

"Twelve thirty."

Brett heard his officer mutter "yes" under his breath. "My wife saw her getting into an old hearse around then. The one the mortician drives on occasion."

Brett's spike pulsed. "Are you sure?"

"Yeah, she passed the vehicle on her way home from volunteering at school."

"Thanks." His visit to Richard would have to wait. "I'll swing by the funeral home." He ended the call and pressed down on the accelerator.

He arrived, parked in front of the door and bolted inside. Maybe she had stopped by here. And maybe the only reason she didn't answer her cell phone was because the battery had died.

Maybe.

Unease twisted his insides.

Derreck stepped out of his office. "I'm going to need you to move the cruiser, Chief Eggert. We are having a wake soon."

"Is Nicole here?" Brett strode through the foyer, toward Nicole's back office.

The confusion on Derreck's face made Brett's stomach drop. Nicole wasn't here.

"Where's Gene?"

"What's going on?"

"Is Gene here?"

"No, he must be running an errand." Derreck pushed his black-framed glasses up on his scrunched nose.

Brett scrubbed a hand across his face and considered his next move. He pulled his cell phone out of his pocket to call Nicole's grandmother and the voice mail indicator caught his attention. His heart leaped in his throat.

Brett called voice mail and listened. Silence. He pressed the phone tighter to his ear. Muffled sounds floated across the line competing with the pulse slamming in his ears.

"…this the peanut trail?" Nicole's voice sounded far away.

"Shut up." Brett didn't recognize the angry male voice. Was it Gene?

"Did you ever ride…" there were some incomprehensible sounds "…the peanut trail?" Brett's heartbeat kicked up a notch. Nicole was trying to tell him her location.

An angry voice was followed by rustling. Then nothing. The line went dead.

Brett pulled the phone away from his ear and looked at it, as if that would give him answers.

Brett turned to Derreck. "Gene picked up Nicole in the hearse and now she's missing."

Derreck shook his head. "No, our hearse is parked out back." He strode into the office and pulled up the blinds. "See?"

Brett scratched his head. "Is there an older hearse?"

Derreck turned up his nose. "Ah, Gene has a thing for cars. My aunt gave him an old hearse that we had stored in the garage." He ran a hand over his thinning hair. He scrunched his shoulders in his pale gray suit. "To each his own, I guess."

"It's a 1972 hearse." Brett spun around. Mr. Peters stood in the doorway leaning on his cane. He tipped his head toward his office. "Come here. I'll show you a photo of it."

Brett followed Mr. Peters to his office. The older gentleman tapped the glass covering his desk. Under it was a photo of a hearse and a young Mrs. Peters. "This. Here."

"Okay. Can you call Gene on his cell phone?" Brett squeezed his own cell. Nicole had left him a message. Something about the peanut trail. He had to get out there.

"Sure." Mr. Peters opened a black book on his desk and looked up Gene's number. "What should I say?"

"Ask him where he is. Tell him you got a death call. That you need him to come into work."

Mr. Peters nodded, then dialed the number. He waited, then mouthed, "Voice mail."

"Leave a message," Brett whispered.

Mr. Peters left the message and ended the call. "What's going on?"

"Nicole's missing and one of my officers saw her getting into the car with Gene."

Mr. Peters lowered himself into his desk chair. It groaned when he leaned back. "I'm sure there's an explanation. She was walking? Perhaps he offered her a ride."

Brett shook his head. "Nicole never made it to her destination. She was supposed to meet with the school principal." Even if the call hadn't really come from the principal.

He checked his phone again. He had to go.

Brett was striding toward the front door when Gene walked in. Brett stopped short. The two men locked gazes and unease wormed down Brett's spine. "Where is Nicole?"

"Nicole?" Darkness flashed in the man's eyes and a smarmy smile curved his lips.

"Yes, someone saw you pick her up."

Gene's features relaxed. "Oh, yeah, I gave her a ride to school." He flicked imaginary lint off his coat sleeve.

"She never showed up." Brett watched Gene carefully, but he was hard to read.

"Well…" Gene ran the tip of his steel-toed shoe along the seam in the carpet. "I dropped her off at the top of Elm Street. She didn't want me to drive the hearse near the school. She thought it might upset the children."

Gene turned to Mr. Peters. "Anything you need me to

do before I run out again? Mrs. Peters asked me to pick up some pastry hearts."

Mr. Peters stammered. "I—I left you a message that we had a death call, but they called back and canceled."

Gene narrowed his gaze at his boss, as if he was trying to read his mind. "That's strange. Did the person not die?" A smirk tugged on the corner of his mouth.

Mr. Peters cast a nervous glance at Brett and Brett said a silent prayer that the elderly man wouldn't crack under pressure.

Mr. Peters cleared his throat. "The hospital said the family had decided to go with a funeral home in Buffalo. Closer to the extended family."

Gene shrugged. "Then I guess I'll go pick up the pastries for Mrs. Peters."

Brett watched Gene leave, burning anger growing in his gut. "Mr. Peters, call your wife. Ask her if she has Gene running errands for her."

For the second time in the span of a few minutes, Brett watched Mr. Peters place a call. After he hung up, he said, "Yes, Martha has him running to the grocery store. She felt like some pastry hearts."

Brett nodded. "Okay." Either way it didn't change the fact that Gene had been the last person to see Nicole.

"If you see Nicole, call me right away." Brett stormed outside and got into his cruiser. He called Ed and told him to follow Gene. Gene was going to lead them to Nicole.

He just knew it.

Meanwhile, Brett drove to the peanut trail. His pulse spiked when he noticed fresh tire tracks in the snow. He turned onto the trail and sent up a quick prayer. Daylight was fading fast.

Brett turned onto the trail and followed the tire tracks. The tracks stopped suddenly. Brett threw the car into Park and climbed out. The snow had been disturbed in a wide space next to the trail. Brett searched the area. No sign of Nicole.

He scratched his head. Did he really think Nicole was going to walk out of the woods? The snow nearest the trees was undisturbed. So it was unlikely Nicole was in the woods.

Brett scanned the ground. Something pink poked out of the snow. He bent down and picked it up.

Nicole's mitten.

Panic had nearly consumed Nicole. She had no idea how long she had been trapped in the inky blackness of the casket. It felt like forever. An eternity.

She drew in shallow breaths. For what seemed like the hundredth time she prayed, *Our Father, who art in heaven...*

Please let Brett find me. Please don't take me away from my son.

Nicole pushed against the satiny top of the casket with the palms of her hands. It didn't budge. A tear trailed down the side of her face. She kicked the top with her boot. Nothing to show for it except aching toes.

Oh, please, dear Lord, help me.

Nicole swallowed hard. Then she froze. Her ears perked up.

"Nicole!"

Her heart raced. Someone was out there. Someone was calling her name. Joy swept over her. She mustered all her energy and screamed. Screamed as loud as she could.

Brett heard a muffled scream. It was coming from the ground. He stopped walking and listened. Pounding replaced the screams.

Brett raced to where he heard the sounds. He dropped to his knees and starting clawing at the snow and branches with his gloved hands. He uncovered sections of a pine box. No, not a box.

A casket.

He worked faster. "Nicole, I'm here. I'm coming. Hold on."

Brett cleared away the branches and the snow. He wrapped his hands around the edges until he found the release and pried the lid open.

Nicole shot up to a seated position and gulped in air. She lifted her eyes heavenward. "Thank you, God."

Brett leaned in and pulled her out. He held her close, breathing in her hair, her being, his sweet relief.

After a moment, he held her at arm's length. "Who did this to you?"

"Gene Gentry. He was going on about how I was mean to him in high school." She rolled her shoulders. "Said he had a job to do." She worked her lower lip. "He wasn't making any sense. I hardly knew him in high school."

"Come on." With an arm around her back, he guided her to his cruiser. He settled her into the vehicle. He leaned across and buckled her in. She shuddered and smiled up at him. He brushed his knuckle across her cool cheek. "Are you okay?"

She raised her eyebrows and smiled. "I'm fantastic." Relief edged her tone. "I never thought I'd be so happy to see snow falling from the sky."

"I'm sorry I didn't protect you from him." Brett cupped her cheek.

"You came when it counted." Nicole covered his hand and leaned into it with her cheek.

Brett kissed her cold nose, then pulled away. "I'm calling the station. I'll have Ed pick up Gene." He ran around the front of the vehicle and climbed in his side.

An alarmed expression swept across her eyes. "Is Ethan okay?"

"He's fine. He's home with Gigi." He offered her his phone. "Call them. You'll all feel better."

Brett started the car and cranked up the heat. He eased the vehicle along the rutted mud tracks on the peanut trail while Nicole talked to Ethan. Warmth coiled around his heart.

Everything was as it should be.

Almost.

Nicole ended the call and put Brett's cell phone in the cup holder on the dash. "Did you find my mitten?"

Brett slowed the vehicle and reached into his jacket pocket and pulled it out. "Yes." He handed it to her. "This mitten didn't just drop, did it?"

Nicole's head was beginning to pound from all the adrenaline that had been pumping through her veins. "I was leaving you a clue." She laughed, a mirthless sound.

"You're one smart lady. Your voice mail about your location was brilliant. I don't know why I didn't hear the call when it came in."

"Well, you heard eventually. That's what counts." Nicole stared at the houses outside the passenger window. Her hometown had never looked so sweet. She absentmindedly ran her finger along the seams of the cold, wet mitten. "My mom made these for herself. It's the only thing from her that I still own."

Brett reached across and squeezed her hand, not knowing what to say. After the moment passed, he asked, "Are you up for going to the station?"

Nicole nodded. "I'm looking forward to putting this behind me."

SIXTEEN

Nicole's heart skittered when she saw Gene. He was sitting on an orange plastic chair in the police station with his hands cuffed in front of him. He rocked back and forth. Back and forth. His eyes were downcast as if the speckles in the gray linoleum were absolutely fascinating.

A bead of sweat dripped down Nicole's back and the gray partitions swayed in her periphery. She was free. She wasn't in the casket anymore. She was free.

She took a deep breath.

Officer Hanson's calm tone sank into her consciousness. He asked Gene a question she couldn't hear and Gene rocked faster. Back and forth. Back and forth.

Nicole gravitated toward the man. With a hand on the small of her back, Brett guided her toward his office, away from Gene. She shook her head. "No, I need to talk to Gene. Figure out what was going on in his head."

"Let us do our job. We'll get to the bottom of this." Brett spoke in a reassuring tone, smoothing the edges of her jangled nerves.

Nicole drew in another deep breath. "I've been running away from things my whole life. I need to face this. I need to know why Gene wanted to kill me." Her raised voice made Ed Hanson swing his gaze toward her. He frowned.

Gene lifted his head and his eyes grew wide. The eyes of a man who had seen a ghost.

"You can't talk to Gene. His lawyer's on the way," Brett whispered into her ear.

Gene rocked faster.

A shuffling sounded from down the hall. Mr. Peters, his wife and Derreck arrived at the station. Derreck was pushing his aunt in a wheelchair.

Mr. Peters leaned heavily on his cane. "Are you okay, Nicole?"

"How did you know we were here?" Brett asked, suspicion making him wary.

Mrs. Peters straightened her rail-thin frame in the wheelchair. "Gene called our home looking for a lawyer. I see he's gotten himself into some sort of trouble." The elderly lady's laserlike glare landed on Gene. "One of the best lawyers is on the way, Gene. A family takes care of their own."

Gene's head snapped up. "I'm sorry—"

Mrs. Peters held up a shaky hand. "Wait for the lawyer."

Gene continued his back-and-forth motion. "I tried to do what you asked, Mrs. Peters."

A shower of icy tingles rained down Nicole's neck and back and solidified in her gut.

"Gene," Mrs. Peters said curtly, "enough of this babbling. A lawyer is coming."

Brett touched Nicole's shoulder and gave her a subtle nod. He crossed the room to Mrs. Peters. "Do you need a lawyer, too, Mrs. Peters?"

The elderly lady picked up a shaky hand in dismissal. "Why would I need a lawyer?" The familiar haughty tone of her voice went right through Nicole.

"Because you asked Gene to hurt Nicole."

Nicole held her breath while Brett talked.

"What is this all about?" Mr. Peters put his hand on his wife's shoulder. "My wife is ill. This is far too much excitement for her." He nudged Derreck out of the way and started to turn the wheelchair around to leave.

"Stop!" Mrs. Peters yelled. Her husband did as he was told.

Mrs. Peters drew herself up as best she could in her wheelchair. "I had nothing to do with this nonsense."

"But…" Gene's lower lip began to quiver "…I tried to get rid of her for you."

Nicole gasped.

"Don't listen to that babbling fool." Mrs. Peters placed one hand on top of the other on the blanket covering her lap. If Brett didn't know better, he would have thought Mrs. Peters was a prim and proper old lady and not the prime suspect in having Nicole buried alive.

Hanson stood and Brett held up his hand to stop him.

"Gene's under a lot of pressure." Mrs. Peters twirled her index finger near her temple. "He's crazy."

Gene drew himself up, his shackled hands clasped in front of him. Darkness swept across his features and his lips, forehead and eyes crumbled in rage. "I am not crazy. I am *not* crazy."

Fear glistened in Mrs. Peters's eyes. "Enough of that, Gene. Enough."

Mr. Peters stood, as if frozen, behind Mrs. Peters's wheelchair.

Gene fisted his hands and his forehead crumbled. He glowered at the elderly lady. "You asked me to kill Nicole to protect you."

Dark rage swept over Mrs. Peters's frail features. "I asked you to make it look like a suicide, you crazy fool. A suicide."

Brett swooped in, grabbed Mr. Peters around the shoulders and guided him toward a chair. He loosened the older man's tie. "Are you okay?"

Mr. Peters held his hand over his heart. "I think I'm having a heart attack."

"Call an ambulance!" Brett hollered over his shoulder. Ed picked up the phone.

Mrs. Peters pursed her lips. "I'm surrounded by weak men." She pounded her fist on her leg. "If my stupid body cooperated, I'd be able to handle things myself. Instead, I have to rely on other people." She shook her head, her features taut. "My father always said, 'If you want a job done right, do it yourself.'"

Derreck flattened himself against the wall and watched the situation unfold.

"Why did you want Gene to hurt me?" Nicole finally spoke up.

Mrs. Peters broke down in a coughing spell. When she recovered, she locked gazes with Nicole. "Because you were the only one who saw what was actually going on." She coughed again. "Do you know how expensive private nurses are? And if you thought for a minute I was going to leave the house my daddy built and move into a stinky old-folks home, you're wrong." Her voice shook. "Dead wrong."

Nicole pressed a kiss to Ethan's head and inhaled the scent of baby shampoo. A few hours ago, she thought she'd never be able to do this again. She pulled his comforter up and smoothed it across his chest.

"Did you say your prayers, little man?" Nicole sat on the edge of the bed.

"I was waiting for you," Ethan said in a sleepy voice.

Nicole started their evening prayer routine and Ethan joined in. When they finished, her son rolled over and tucked his hand under the pillow. "'Night, Mom. Love you."

"I love you, too."

Nicole slipped out of the bedroom and pulled the door closed. She was surprised to find Brett waiting for her in the kitchen. Gigi smiled. "I'm going to bed now, too. It's been a long day."

"'Night, Gigi."

"'Night." Gigi turned her gaze toward Brett. "Thank you. Thank you for bringing Nicole home to us."

Brett gave her a slight nod. "My pleasure."

Gigi disappeared into her bedroom. Nicole sat and let out a heavy sigh. "I'm surprised to see you here. I thought you'd be busy wrapping up all the loose ends."

He reached out and brushed his thumb across her cheek, leaving a trail of warmth coiling from her cheek and straight to her heart. "I needed to see you."

Nicole narrowed her gaze, confused.

"I just wanted to say good-night. Reassure myself you were still okay."

She held out her hands, palms up. "I'm wonderful. Thanks to you." She shook her head. "I still can't believe Mrs. Peters wanted Gene to kill me."

"You had scratched the surface of the embezzlement scheme and she was afraid you'd uncover more. Days before Missy's fatal accident, Gene had overheard you talking on the phone with the King family. Gave him enough time to plant the jewelry in your jacket. He was Mrs. Peters's eyes and ears at the funeral home."

Nicole let out a frustrated huff. "Gene harbored resentment toward me before Mrs. Peters recruited him to get rid of me. It made her job easier, I imagine."

She touched his hand. "How is Mr. Peters? Do you think he was involved?"

"He's resting at the hospital. I think Mr. Peters had an inkling something was going on, but he loves his wife. He'd do anything to protect her. I think that's why he settled so quickly with the King family. Everything will come out in the investigation."

"What about Derreck? He should have known better."

"My gut tells me Derreck had no idea what was going on." Brett cupped her elbow. "You were the real threat."

"And the perfect scapegoat."

"Exactly. Mrs. Peters decided to use your past against you."

Nicole shook her head. "She had Gene plant jewelry to make me seem untrustworthy. Guilty. The level of detail was amazing, even setting me up at the pawnshops."

"We're just scratching the surface, but apparently, Mrs. Peters is adept at forging signatures. She had a lot of time on her hands. She changed the contracts on prearrangements and stole money from the clients. She had Gene slip new contracts into the files. If a client complained, Mr. Peters automatically smoothed things over. Mrs. Peters is a force to be reckoned with. Unfortunately, I believe we'll find most clients never knew they had been cheated. When you started asking questions, Mrs. Peters got rattled."

Nicole rubbed the back of her neck. "Lucky me."

"And it turns out Richard White was telling the truth."

"I guess some people can change." She smiled up at Brett, but her thoughts were still racing trying to put together the pieces of the puzzle. "Gene ran my car off the road trying to kill me. He tried again with the icicles. Why didn't he try again in the bowling alley bathroom? Why just scare me?" She ran her hand slowly up her arm, stifling a shudder.

"Gene's not rational. I think he took pleasure in taunting you. I think that's why Mrs. Peters was able to recruit him. He claims he didn't like you going all the way back to high school."

Nicole slowly shook his head. "I never knew."

"I'm sure you never intentionally hurt him." Brett tilted his head, kindness radiating from his eyes.

"I'm not blaming myself, but I think we often forget how a little kindness can go a long way."

"Can you ever forgive me?"

Nicole jerked her head back. "Why?"

"For ever doubting you, even just a little. I knew in my heart you were innocent all along, but I had been burned before…"

"By your brother."

Brett swallowed hard and nodded.

"We've both come a long way in learning to trust."

Nicole bowed her head briefly. "I feel like the weight of the world has been lifted from my shoulders." She met his gaze. "I'm glad I finally stuck around long enough to trust someone." She paused. "I'm glad I trusted you."

EPILOGUE

"Can I get you ladies anything else?" Nicole grabbed a soda from the cooler. Gigi and Mrs. Eggert sat next to each other in lawn chairs a few feet away from the picnic table where remnants of an early spring picnic sat on a gingham tablecloth.

"That was a lovely lunch. Thank you." Mrs. Eggert held up her cup of tea. "You thought of everything."

"That's my Nicole. She's a good girl." Gigi touched Nicole's hand. She squeezed her grandmother's hand in return.

Mrs. Eggert's gaze landed on Nicole. "Yes, she is. I'm sorry I was so hard on you. I couldn't see past my grief at losing Max." This wasn't the first time Brett's mother had expressed her feelings.

"I know." Nicole stood and lightly touched Mrs. Eggert's shoulder. "I understand." And this wasn't the first time Nicole had accepted her apology. She figured Brett's mother had to work her way through her grief. Mr. Eggert, on the other hand, apologized once and moved on, choosing to show his contrition through kind acts toward her and her son.

Mrs. Eggert shook her head and pressed a fist to her chest. "No, it was no excuse. I could have lost out on ever knowing my grandson. Ethan is such a joy."

"That he is." Nicole laughed. "I better head to the dock and see how they're doing." She tented her hand over her eyes. The midafternoon sun glistened off the ripples in the pond.

"Tell George not to stay out too long. He tires easily." Mrs. Eggert tapped the arm of Gigi's chair. Her grandmother had made wonderful strides in her health and was now using a cane instead of a wheelchair. "He had chemo two weeks ago and it really takes a lot out of him."

Nicole smiled and strolled down the grassy incline. The warm sun felt awesome on her face after a long winter. Brett crouched next to Ethan at the end of the dock, fastening his life jacket.

Mr. Eggert was already in the rowboat, smiling in his bright orange vest. He held on to the side of the dock to prevent the rowboat—his life's work—from drifting away.

"Want to come with us, Mom?" Ethan danced on the balls of his feet while Brett fastened the final buckle.

Nicole waved her hands in front of her. "Not today."

Brett patted the orange life vest. "You're all set."

"Thanks, Uncle Brett." Ethan threw his arms around Brett's waist. The pair had become inseparable these past few months. Almost as inseparable as she and Brett. Warmth filled her heart.

"I've never been out in a rowboat before." Ethan smiled brightly. Two new teeth had sprouted through his top gums. Her little man.

Brett held Ethan's hand and guided him into the rowboat. He settled down onto the perfectly sanded seat and wrapped his little hands around the handles of the oars.

"I think Grandpa's going to have to do the rowing, right, Dad?" Brett said.

His father smiled and smoothed his hand along the side of the rowboat. "I never thought I'd get this baby out on the water." He nodded, a look of approval—a sense of accomplishment—on his weathered features.

"You okay?" Brett asked.

"Never been better." Mr. Eggert had lost some weight these past few months, but other than that, he said he felt good. Nicole suspected meeting his grandson had given him a new lease on life. Holding on to the edge of the rowboat, Mr. Eggert maneuvered around to sit next to his grandson. "You can help me row." He dipped the far oar into the water and used the other one to shove off from the dock.

Brett and Nicole stood silently watching grandfather and grandson row across the sun-dappled lake. Brett turned toward Nicole and smiled. She glanced at the older women. If their hand gestures were any indication, the two women were engrossed in a lighthearted discussion.

Brett stepped in front of her, blocking her view. He tipped her face up with a finger under her chin. "A penny for your thoughts."

Nicole smiled coyly. "I have my own penny, thank you very much."

"Glad the job's going well."

"Who knew I'd still want to work at the funeral home after everything that's been going on? Derreck seems to be coming into his own now. He's not a bad boss." Nicole got a sense of satisfaction from helping people in their time of need. "Mr. Peters still comes in a few hours a day. He personally went through all the files and made restitution to anyone who was bilked by his wife. He regrets overlooking his wife's misdeeds, but I'm glad the district attorney's office didn't find reason to press charges against him. I think making restitution has given him a purpose since Mrs. Peters passed away."

"Perhaps that was a blessing. I couldn't imagine Mrs. Peters in jail." Brett traced Nicole's jawline.

Nicole took a step back and stuffed her hands into the back pockets of her jeans. "I can't imagine Gene faring very well."

"He made his own choice."

"Mrs. Peters manipulated him." She squinted toward

the water. "I can't believe the measures she had Gene take. Poor Missy. She'd still be alive if she hadn't borrowed my car."

"Don't blame yourself." Brett's deep voice washed over her.

"Mrs. Peters had to know she'd be discovered eventually."

"She was ill. She only had to keep things quiet for a little longer. She despised the notion of going into a nursing home."

Nicole placed her hand on Brett's chest. Warm. Solid. Dependable. "Missy was an innocent victim."

"You were an innocent victim, too. You have to stop blaming yourself for things you can't control." He covered her hand with his.

"Like your brother."

Brett nodded. "Like my brother." She looked into his warm brown eyes. "I've learned to forgive myself, too." He leaned over and feathered a kiss across her nose. "And there's something else I learned about myself."

Nicole scrunched up her face in confusion. "What?"

"I love you." He tilted his head and pressed his forehead against hers. "And I want to spend the rest of my life with you. You. Me. Ethan."

Tendrils of emotion—deep contentment, love, happiness—swirled around her heart.

Brett brushed a thumb across the back of her hand, sending tingles shooting up her arm. He smiled. "I have something for you." He dug into his pocket and pulled out a gorgeous diamond ring.

Heat flooded her cheeks and her heart raced. Rendered speechless with emotion, she got up on her tiptoes and kissed him. He wrapped his arm around her waist and pulled her closer. He pulled back from the kiss and got down on one knee. "Will you marry me?"

Covering her broad smile with a shaky hand, she cried. Happy tears.

Brett stood and slipped the ring onto her finger and tipped his head in question.

Nicole threw her arms around his neck. "Yes! Yes, I'll marry you."

Brett pulled Nicole close again. "Are you okay with staying in Silver Lake?"

"Yes." She nodded slowly, scanning the lake and smiling when she saw Ethan talking animatedly to his grandfather.

Drawing in a deep breath, Nicole rested her head on Brett's chest. "I feel so content. So happy not to have to live with…" She struggled to put her feelings into words. "I don't know…"

"Secrets?"

"Yeah." Nicole lifted her head and stared into the glittery lake reflecting in Brett's eyes. "No more secrets."

* * * * *

Look for Alison Stone's next book, PLAIN PERIL, on sale in February 2015. You'll find it wherever Love Inspired Suspense books are sold!

Dear Reader,

I hope you enjoyed *Silver Lake Secrets*, my "funeral home book." Like most of my story ideas, this one has been percolating a long time. When I was fourteen years old, my older sister enrolled in the mortuary science program at SUNY Canton. During her first internship at a local funeral home, she'd come home and share stories around the dinner table. I'd feel horrible for the children of the couple killed while riding a motorcycle and my stomach would turn when she described the embalming process. Lucky me. Why couldn't she have gone to school for tourism or something?

I could never be a funeral director. (I prefer this title to mortician or undertaker.) I am extremely squeamish by nature, yet I was fascinated by my sister's new career. She was drawn to the job because she wanted to help the families of the deceased during this very difficult time. How many people are in a position to do that?

When people found out I was writing a book about a funeral home they offered to connect me with a friend of a friend who knew a funeral director. I'd smile and tell them I had my own connection. So thanks, Annie, for answering my questions (for example, can a person climb into a casket while in the back of a hearse? Why, yes!) and giving me great ideas for the plot. I am in awe of your career choices and proud to call you my sister.

And, readers, I hoped you enjoyed the unique setting for my latest Harlequin Love Inspired Suspense. The beauty of being a writer is the flexibility to explore careers and settings that I may never have otherwise. Where shall I explore next?

Live, love, laugh,
Alison Stone

Questions for Discussion

1. We all make mistakes. The heroine, Nicole, made some bad decisions in her youth and ended up being a teenage mother. Yet she now considers her son as one of her greatest blessings. Have you ever made a bad decision that turned out to be a blessing in disguise?

2. Nicole faced a lot of hardships in her young life, yet she clung to her faith. Is this surprising? Have you ever had your faith tested?

3. The hero's family blamed Nicole for Max's death. She was the last one to see him before he drove off and wrapped his car around a tree while impaired by drugs. Was it fair to blame her? Is it understandable?

4. We are taught to honor our fathers and mothers. Mrs. Eggert, Brett's mother, can't seem to get past her anger at Nicole and doesn't want Brett to get involved with her. Brett has to look past his own hurt, and his mother's, to help Nicole. Have you ever had a conflict with your parents about doing what you thought was right? How did you resolve this conflict?

5. Nicole's career as a mortuary cosmetologist is unique. Could you ever do her job? (Interesting fact: Many funeral directors perform all the tasks necessary to prepare the body for burial, from embalming to makeup, and do not hire a separate cosmetologist.)

6. The villain is trying to set up Nicole by planting jewelry from the deceased in ways that will implicate her. Do you think a family should bury a sentimental or

expensive piece of jewelry with their deceased loved one? Or do you think the piece should stay with the family? What happens when the family's wishes conflict with the wishes of the deceased?

7. Brett had many hostile exchanges with his brother before he died. Now he lives with that guilt. Have you ever lost a loved one? Do you recall your last conversation?

8. As a follow-up to question six, do you make a habit of parting on good terms with those you love?

9. *Silver Lake Secrets* is set in snowy Western New York. Do you have a preference for the season in which a book is set?

10. The issue of elder care is a recurring theme in this story. Nicole has returned to Silver Lake to care for her aging grandma. Also, Mr. Peters, the owner of the funeral home, is caring for his ailing wife. Have you had experience caring for an aging loved one? How has it affected your life?

11. Brett's parents end up reconciling with Nicole and are able to meet their grandson. Have you ever had an opportunity to look past hurt in order to receive a greater blessing?

12. There are safeguards set up to protect people from embezzlement in the funeral home industry, but every so often a case surfaces in the news. Have you ever heard about any crimes committed by funeral home employees?

13. Brett grows in faith, in part by being influenced by Nicole's strong faith despite her circumstances. What life experiences have helped you grow in faith?

14. Nicole's life is threatened when Gene buries her alive. Confined to a dark, small space is one of my worst nightmares. What are you afraid of?

15. In the end, the Eggert and Braun families reconcile. Mr. Eggert, Brett's father, is frail as he battles cancer, but meeting his grandson has given him a new lease on life. In a way, his illness expedited the reconciliation. None of us has any guarantee of a tomorrow. What are you putting off today? Why?

REQUEST YOUR FREE BOOKS!

2 FREE RIVETING INSPIRATIONAL NOVELS
PLUS 2 FREE MYSTERY GIFTS

Love Inspired®
SUSPENSE

YES! Please send me 2 FREE Love Inspired® Suspense novels and my 2 FREE mystery gifts (gifts are worth about $10). After receiving them, if I don't wish to receive any more books, I can return the shipping statement marked "cancel." If I don't cancel, I will receive 4 brand-new novels every month and be billed just $4.74 per book in the U.S. or $5.24 per book in Canada. That's a savings of at least 21% off the cover price. It's quite a bargain! Shipping and handling is just 50¢ per book in the U.S. and 75¢ per book in Canada.* I understand that accepting the 2 free books and gifts places me under no obligation to buy anything. I can always return a shipment and cancel at any time. Even if I never buy another book, the two free books and gifts are mine to keep forever.

123/323 IDN F5AC

Name	(PLEASE PRINT)

Address	Apt. #

City	State/Prov.	Zip/Postal Code

Signature (if under 18, a parent or guardian must sign)

Mail to the **Harlequin® Reader Service:**
IN U.S.A.: P.O. Box 1867, Buffalo, NY 14240-1867
IN CANADA: P.O. Box 609, Fort Erie, Ontario L2A 5X3

**Are you a current subscriber to Love Inspired Suspense books
and want to receive the larger-print edition?
Call 1-800-873-8635 or visit www.ReaderService.com.**

* Terms and prices subject to change without notice. Prices do not include applicable taxes. Sales tax applicable in N.Y. Canadian residents will be charged applicable taxes. Offer not valid in Quebec. This offer is limited to one order per household. Not valid for current subscribers to Love Inspired Suspense books. All orders subject to credit approval. Credit or debit balances in a customer's account(s) may be offset by any other outstanding balance owed by or to the customer. Please allow 4 to 6 weeks for delivery. Offer available while quantities last.

Your Privacy—The Harlequin® Reader Service is committed to protecting your privacy. Our Privacy Policy is available online at www.ReaderService.com or upon request from the Harlequin Reader Service.
We make a portion of our mailing list available to reputable third parties that offer products we believe may interest you. If you prefer that we not exchange your name with third parties, or if you wish to clarify or modify your communication preferences, please visit us at www.ReaderService.com/consumerchoice or write to us at Harlequin Reader Service Preference Service, P.O. Box 9062, Buffalo, NY 14269. Include your complete name and address.

LIS13R

SPECIAL EXCERPT FROM

Love Inspired.
SUSPENSE

*SWAT team member Isaac Morrison didn't plan to
fall for his best friend's sister. But when Leah Nichols
and her son are in trouble, he'll stop at nothing to
keep them out of harm's way.*

Read on for a sneak peek of
UNDER THE LAWMAN'S PROTECTION
by Laura Scott

"Stay down. I'm going to go make sure there isn't someone out there."

"Wait!" Leah cried as Isaac was about to open his car
door. "Don't go. Stay here with us."

He was torn between two impossible choices. If someone had shot out the tires on purpose, he couldn't just
wait for that person to come finish them off. Nor did he
want to leave Leah and Ben here alone.

So far he wasn't doing the greatest job of keeping
Hawk's sister and her son safe. If he'd been wearing his
bulletproof gear he would be in better shape to go out to
investigate.

Isaac peered out the window, trying to see if anyone
was out there. Sitting here was making him crazy, so he
decided doing something was better than nothing.

"I'm armed, Leah, so don't worry about me. I promise
I'll do whatever it takes to keep you and Ben safe."

He could tell she wanted to protest, but she bit her lip
and nodded. She pulled her son out of his booster seat

LISEXP1214

and tucked him next to her so that he was protected on either side. Then she curled her body around him. The fact that she would risk herself to protect Ben gave Isaac a funny feeling in the center of his chest.

Leah's actions were humbling. He hadn't been attracted to a woman in a long time, not since his wife had left him.

But this wasn't the time to ruminate over the past. Isaac's ex-wife and son were gone, and nothing in the world would bring them back. So Isaac would do the next best thing—protect Leah and Ben with his life if necessary.

Don't miss
UNDER THE LAWMAN'S PROTECTION
by Laura Scott,
available January 2015 wherever
Love Inspired® Suspense books and ebooks are sold.